MW00907358

IS THERE AN ACTOR IN THE HOUSE?

IS THERE AN ACTOR IN THE HOUSE?

Dramatic Material from Pantomime to Play

VIRGINIA BRADLEY

DODD, MEAD & COMPANY
NEW YORK

These plays may be used for live performances which are not given for profit, without permission.

Copyright © 1975 by Virginia Jonas Bradley
All rights reserved
No part of this book may be reproduced in any form without permission in writing from the publisher
Printed in the United States of America
4 5 6 7 8 9 10

Bradley, Virginia, date
Is there an actor in the house?

SUMMARY: Brief discussions of stage, cast, props, costumes, rehearsals, and improvisation accompany scripts for pantomines, puppet plays, variety programs, skits, and one-act plays.

1. Children's plays. [1. Plays. 2. Amateur theatricals] I. Title.
PN6120.A5B6568 812'.5'4 75–11432
ISBN 0–396–07193–7
ISBN 0-396-08637-3 (pbk.)

To Stephen, Michael, Betty and Patricia,
for whom many of these plays were written.
And to Jerry, *sine qua non.*

"He who has not laughter from the days of his youth, has not life, nor peace, nor any taste of heaven."

"Actors all, we wait in the wings—each in his own time—each to his own role."

CONTENTS

PART IV
THE VARIETY PROGRAM
. . . everyone for himself . . .

PART V
THE SKETCH
. . . pick up your cue . . .

PART VI
THE PLAY
. . . *all together now* . . .

PART VII
IMPROVISATION
. . . *no planning ahead* . . .

PART I

LET'S PUT ON A SHOW

LET'S PUT ON A SHOW

. . . and the fun begins . . .

What kind of a play are you looking for? Something without many lines to learn or maybe no lines at all? Do you want a sketch for Thanksgiving or the first day of spring? You can, of course, thumb through the table of contents and turn directly to the page that interests you. However, why not linger here awhile? Dangle your toes in the water at the edge of the pool before you plunge in. There are suggestions in these first pages that might be useful when the water goes over your head.

The Stage

Where are you going to have the show? In a recreation hall? A gym? What kind of a stage do you have? A big one with footlights and a red velvet curtain? Fine. Your play will have dignity with proper backdrops and room in the wings for the actors who are waiting to go on. You will get the feel of the professional.

On the other hand you may have only a raised platform, a flat gym floor, or even the front of a classroom. No matter. The play's the thing.

Of course, if you don't have a real stage, you probably won't have a curtain, but there are several things you can do about that. Many theatrical companies perform "in the round," on an open stage with the audience on three or even four sides of them. Sometimes they use blackouts when they wish to change the set or indicate the passage of time, but often the actors exit at the end of a scene, and the audience is allowed to see what goes on between the acts. Maybe you will want to try one of these methods.

There are other tricks. You can rig up a curtain with flag standards or clothes racks and old drapes or blankets that members of the cast can pull back and forth across the stage space. Or if you want something very simple, use signs: THE CURTAIN IS OPEN . . . THE CURTAIN IS CLOSED. Signs are always good for a laugh. You'll see. Where the play is given is not important—*how* it is given is what counts.

Picking a Play

When it comes to selecting a play there is a very slim chance of your finding one that is exactly what you are looking for. Unless a script has been written especially for your group, it may have to be changed a little.

Suppose you want something for Washington's birthday. The selection in this book, *Better Luck Tomorrow, Mr. Washington,* may sound just about right. It's short and there aren't too many lines to learn. Nor does it need elaborate staging. But you have six boys and what are you going to do about Martha? No problem at all. Have one of the boys dress up in a costume of the period, with full skirt and ruffled morning cap. The audience might wonder who in the world it is, and you'll add an element of mystery to your production.

Of course you may have all girls and the skit you would really like to use seems to call for boys. The same turnabout can be made. Let the girls dress up, drag their voices down, and walk with a longer stride. Some of the sketches here have been deliberately planned for shifting roles.

Suppose you find a play that is perfect, except that there are only six characters and you have eight people to use. Put another tourist in the crowd, another rider on the roller coaster. Give him a line if he wants it or at least a colorful costume. Perhaps a few members of your group would rather not perform at all but just want to help. They can be the stagehands, the curtain pullers.

If the play calls for more people than you have, characters could be left out or maybe some of the cast could double and take two parts. Usually there's someone willing to do that since it would mean extra glory.

Don't decide a skit is wrong for you until you have looked at it closely. With a little imagination you can probably push it into your own scheme. Naturally you will avoid picking a play that is simply out of the question, but if it's only a matter of too many lines to learn, remember that many of those lines can be given to a narrator—that lucky fellow who can memorize anything or at least read as though he enjoys it.

Don't be afraid to move the speeches around either, adding and subtracting to suit your actors and their talents. And by all means substitute your own words if it will bring the play up to date. Language is fickle. The "in" way of saying something today may be "out" tomorrow.

The Cast

Certainly anybody who wants to be in the show should have the chance, but common sense will tell you that if Susan can't remember where the rehearsal was to be held, she's not going to do very well as the star of your drama. A part just cannot go to someone because he wants it, or even because he seems at first to be made for it. Pete might be the smallest fellow in your group and would look ridiculously perfect in his father's top coat. But if Pete's voice doesn't carry across the room, it certainly won't reach the back row.

Or maybe there's Mark who has a booming voice when he's sitting around in a circle at the meetings. He doesn't even seem to have trouble learning lines. But if Mark stammers when he gets up to talk he'll probably freeze on the stage and never be able to say a word.

Remember also that the longest part isn't always the best. Many times the character who simply walks on stage without opening his mouth is the one who brings down the house. The rabbit who pickets the vegetable patch carrying a sign, THIS GARDEN UNFAIR TO A HARE. The player who has supposedly fallen asleep before it was time for his appearance and is carried onto the stage for the curtain call. This fellow doesn't even have to walk—you can be sure he'll get applause.

Have tryouts, let everyone read for the part he likes, but don't decide anything right away. Hold some practice sessions before the cast is definitely chosen. Invite outsiders. Find out how people hold up in front of an audience. You don't want hurt feelings, so talk about the things that could happen and reach an agreement. Everyone wants this to be a good show.

Props, Costumes, and Make-up

Let's assume you now have the play and the cast and you know where you are going to perform. Don't bother about bulky scenery. Most of the plays in this book are very short and it is foolish to spend time and energy pushing a sofa around or dragging in a piano. The announcer or narrator can tell the audience what the scene is. And there are always the signs—if the action takes place at the airport or a park, put up a poster announcing the fact.

Exaggerate everything. Let the detective carry an enormous ledger instead of a notebook and a magnifying glass the size of a dinner plate. A good prop trick will often be better than the real thing. The stone that is turned over may not actually be visible from the back of the room, but if you hang a label on it in foot high letters, the audience will get the idea and the humor too.

The costumes can depend on imagination also. Again exaggerate; make everything bigger than life. The curled paper beard of an old man can be as long as the patience of the paper curler. If the character wears glasses, make them saucer-like—out of a wire coathanger perhaps.

The circus fat man offers great possibilities and the two-headed boy can be a challenge to the whole cast. Suggestions are given at the end of the circus play in this book, but think of how you would handle it. You might have a better idea.

You don't have to spend money. Look in attics and garages and on closet shelves. With a little thought you can come up with almost anything.

Make use of color too. Great splashes of it. Let the clown wear red and yellow and green. A king should have purple, or maybe not—perhaps you have a king who likes pink. That might be fun to explain.

Make-up isn't all-important. If there is someone available who knows about face liners, spirit gum, and crepe hair, that's fine. Powder to change brown hair to gray and a few lines with an eyebrow pencil will transform youth to age, and if eight-year-old Bonnie walks with a slow step, wears a shawl, and carries a cane, the audience will know her for the old lady she's supposed to be.

Rehearsals

In putting your show together, you may discover that you'll have the greatest hassle with the rehearsals. One person ought to be in charge, and if there is no adult involved, then someone from the group should be selected. Perhaps you found the right person back there when you were casting. At any rate, there should be unanimous agreement on one who will be fair but firm.

After you have your leader, discuss the show. Read the script. If someone has a good idea which should be used, put it in. Get everyone's approval. Then rehearse again and again. Short periods, maybe, but often.

It will become boring to say the same lines over and over and go through the same actions until they seem stupid. But remember the audience will see and hear the play just once, and that's the whole point. Be sure your performance is the best you can make it.

Of course you can have refreshments, but not until you have finished the rehearsing. You might also think about having a party after the show has been presented. It can be a real celebration if everything comes off right. That promise should keep people on their toes even if the glory of success doesn't.

Something must be said about preparing for emergencies. Vacations and broken legs have a way of interfering with the best of plans. Try to have someone around who can pinch hit. There's always somebody who knows everybody's lines. Maybe he could double. Or remember those two who decided they'd rather pull the curtain? Could you get them to change their minds? A solution will pop up. How can you possibly call off the performance after all the work you've put into it? The show must go on. Those aren't just idle words.

One Special Word about Puppets

This is a book of plays; it is not a book on puppetry. You will find all sorts of information at the library on making various kinds of puppets and constructing theaters for them. Still, since puppet plays are included here, it seems only fair to provide you with some suggestions.

Your first question is undoubtedly, "What will we use for a stage?" Many puppet shows have been presented from behind a card table turned on its side and draped. You will do without a curtain in this case, and your show will be on the simplest level.

An alternative, however, is not difficult to put together. Find a large packing box (a refrigerator carton is ideal) and cut the stage opening out of the top half of one side. Paint or decorate the bottom half as you wish. Someone may volunteer to make a curtain which can be operated like drapes with a single pull, but you can always hang pieces of old sheeting or muslin on twine or wire and push them open or closed by hand.

Remove the back panel of the packing case and spread the sides out at an angle to give the puppeteers more space to conceal themselves. They will, of course, be crouched beneath the stage opening. You can have a backdrop scene if you wish, which can be fastened to the sides of the box above the operators' heads.

You are in luck if your puppet theater can be set up on a real stage with a curtain that can be drawn just to the sides of the packing box. This will allow greater freedom for the puppeteers to move in and out of position. It may also, of course, add the problem of being heard if the great open stage is behind the performers. They will have to speak up.

The puppets themselves offer a number of possibilities. The plays in this book were written with hand puppets in mind, the kind that fit over the fingers and are limited to movement of arms and head.

You can cut patterns for hands, body, and head from brown wrapping paper. Then, using the patterns, cut the pieces from muslin in pairs. The head can be just two round sections with the features painted on if you wish, but profiles offer greater interest. You can make the most of a long nose, a high forehead, a chin that sticks out.

Stitch the pairs together and stuff the hands and head with cotton. If the stuffing is packed well, the face will take on width. The mouth and eyes can be painted or put on with crayon, and the hair can be fashioned of yarn. Finally, attach the head and hands to the body section, adding whatever details of costume you wish—a ruffled collar, a tie, a hat.

If all this is more of a job than you want, then use the simplest dolls of all: paper bags. Stuff them with cotton for the head, making it secure with string around the neck; paint the face; attach yarn hair. Cut holes in the sides of the sack for fingers which will provide the puppet's hands. It doesn't take much to make an audience believe, but if you do spend time and effort on good puppets you can use them over and over again in other skits.

You've stayed here long enough. You must be getting impatient to dive in, and the fun all lies ahead. Most of these plays have been produced by young people from seven to twelve, but age is not important. Get to work. There's a lot to do before someone says in a hoarse stage whisper, "O.K. now. Everybody ready? *Curtain going up!*"

PART II

PANTOMIME

PANTOMIME

. . . let's have no talking here . . .

Although it has its roots far back in the past, pantomime in its present-day sense means simply action without words.

If there are no words, there are no lines to learn. If there are no lines to learn, there is less work. Logical conclusion: why not make your first play a pantomime?

Keep in mind, however, that if the actors do not talk, then their movements become more important. Each shake of the hand, each nod of the head, each sweep of the arm must be magnified.

The great pantomimists, of course, perform without any props, or costumes, or even sound effects, but there is no need for you to give up these things. You will depend on them to get your story across.

Remember, mum's the word now.

AT THE SATURDAY MATINEE

CHARACTERS

THE ANNOUNCER

THE USHER

AN OLD MAN

PRE-TEENERS, TWO OR MORE

THE SHOPPER

THE GRANDMOTHER

THE MOTHER

THE CHILDREN, AS MANY AS DESIRED

Create a theater within a theater by setting up posters to the left and the right of the closed curtain. THE MAJESTIC SPECIAL SHOWING . . . THE MONSTER'S REVENGE . . . TODAY ONLY. *The* ANNOUNCER *enters from the right.*

ANNOUNCER. Well, ladies and gentlemen, you can see where we are today, and without keeping you waiting any longer, we'll go inside. Not to watch the show though . . . (*he indicates the posters*) . . . at least not this show. Come on. You'll see what I mean.

(*The* ANNOUNCER *exits as the curtain opens to reveal unoccupied chairs, arranged in rows facing the audience. Somewhere out in front of them is the imaginary screen.*)

A movie house is usually dark and, even though the stage lights are on, the USHER *enters with a flashlight to direct an* OLD MAN *to a seat down front. The* USHER, *of course, is accustomed to the blackness, but the* OLD MAN *squints and blinks in an effort to adjust to his surroundings and feels his way along.*

After he is settled the PRE-TEENERS *come in with a rush, not waiting for assistance. Their hands are filled with popcorn, candy bars, and paper cups. They sit far at the back.*

The USHER *comes in again with a* SHOPPER *who has been shopping all morning. She is laden with packages that crunch and crackle, and like the* OLD MAN *she chooses the front row. Stumbling over him, because she can't see a thing, she transfers her bundles from arm to arm and finally stuffs some of them under the seat and piles the rest on her lap. She leans back with a sigh.*

The sedate little GRANDMOTHER *comes in carrying an oversize satchel and a popsicle, and a young* MOTHER *is pulled down the aisle by three or four lively* CHILDREN. *They all take places somewhere in the middle.*

From this point on each individual has his moment. If a spotlight is available you can use it to direct the audience's attention where you want it, but the same effect can be achieved by a stopping of all movement on the stage except for that of the player whose turn it is to act.

The PRE-TEENERS *giggle, pop their bubble gum, eat, and whisper. Their voices are not heard, of course. Shifting about from one seat to another, they step on people's feet and bump the heads of those in front of them.*

The GRANDMOTHER *turns around to quell the disturbance and all eyes are on her. She glares at the offenders; then she resumes her interest in the picture, wide-eyed, expressing her reaction to the scenes of suspense and terror. She clutches her heart, covers her mouth, adjusts her glasses. She might even take her glasses off and clean them with an enormous white handkerchief from her old-fashioned satchel.*

The OLD MAN *picks up his cameo spot with a loud snore. He has fallen asleep and makes explosive nasal noises. (Even in pantomime noises like this are allowable as sound effects.)*

The young CHILDREN *squirm and climb about on and off their* MOTHER*'s lap. She takes each one of them in turn down the aisle for a drink of water, a trip to the restroom, or a purchase at the refreshment bar. While she is gone there is squabbling among the others, and each time she returns she has trouble settling her brood.*

The SHOPPER *arranges her sacks and boxes again. She has kicked off her shoes and tries to recapture them, probing with her toes. Her packages fall and must be retrieved.*

As a kind of finale the entire group is in motion, reacting to the climax on the screen. One girl shrieks, and the OLD MAN *wakes up with a snort and applauds with great gusto as the curtain falls.*

(When the curtain is closed, the ANNOUNCER *enters again.)*

ANNOUNCER. There you have it, ladies and gentlemen. You have attended the Saturday Matinee where the entertainment on the screen is often topped by that in front of it. Come again sometime when your spirits need a lift. The movie may be disappointing, but look around you. You'll get your money's worth all the same.

Suggestions

The characters here dictate the costuming, and appropriate outfits can certainly be assembled out of any home closet. It might be fun to give the grandmother an old-fashioned hat which she refuses to take off. The hair of the two old people can be grayed with powder, and eyebrow pencil lines will age their faces.

Some of the props are indicated in the script but more may be added. The old man can have a cane or an umbrella, and the children might carry dolls and toys. Just be sure that there are plenty of bundles for the shopper. You can use real food if you wish. It will add to the reality of the situation.

If someone wants to be in the show but doesn't want to act, just have him seated in the theater when the curtain goes up. He can be any character he wishes, but the focus of attention will never be on him.

HELP!

Characters

THE MARCHERS, AS MANY AS DESIRED

THE GIRL

HER FRIEND

THE TREES, AS MANY AS YOU WISH

THE GIRL SCOUT

The MARCHERS *enter in front of the closed curtain. They carry signs:* PROTECT THE MEADOW, PROTECT THE FOREST, PROTECT THE MOUNTAIN. *When they exit, the curtain opens to disclose an almost bare stage. There is a sign on a kind of easel at the left,* THE MEADOW. *There is a litter can or basket at the center back.*

The GIRL *and her* FRIEND *enter left. One of them carries a radio and books; the other has a picnic basket which she opens and unpacks. She spreads a cloth and puts out a milk carton, cups, and several paper sacks. She takes fruit out of the sacks and brings the discard to the litter basket along with other papers that previous picnickers have left behind.*

As the GIRLS *settle themselves, the audience sees them brush away flies and flick away the ants. There is the buzzing of bees which gets louder and louder. One* GIRL *waves away those that bother her, and her* FRIEND *ducks and dodges, apparently trying to avoid others. Suddenly one* GIRL *grabs at her nose, and the other rubs her ear. (They have been stung.) Quickly they gather up the picnic things and run off. (Curtain closes.)*

The MARCHERS *come on again, this time from the back of the auditorium. They march back and forth across the stage in front of the curtain showing their signs and then exit as the curtain opens. The sign has been changed to* THE FOREST, *and the* TREES *fill the stage.*

The GIRLS *enter from the left again, picking their way along the path. Both of them have Band-Aids covering their bee stings. They seem to be studying the trees and they carry books which they refer to as they walk. Suddenly the* TREES *bend down to them, scratch at their faces and their backs. Just before they get to the right exit a* GIRL SCOUT *enters from the left and posts a second sign under the forest one:* WATCH OUT FOR POISON IVY. *The* GIRLS *look down at their ankles, make gestures of despair, and exit. (Curtain closes.)*

The MARCHERS *come on again doing their thing, and when they exit the curtain opens to show that the sign has been changed once more. It now reads* THE MOUNTAIN. *There is another sign at the center of the stage which is turned so that the audience cannot see what it says.*

The GIRLS *enter, both with walking sticks and with packs on their backs. They have more Band-Aids on their faces and their legs and arms are wrapped in gauze. They look a little discouraged, and every few minutes they stop to scratch. They are obviously climbing, and the ascent is steep. They lean forward and huff and puff with effort. Finally they straighten up. They have reached the sign. When they turn it around, the audience can see that it says* THE PEAK. *Both* GIRLS *shout (in pantomime, of course) and jump about in delight, but something gives way under their feet and they lose their balance and fall, rolling and tumbling until they are offstage right.* (*Curtain closes.*)

The MARCHERS *enter a final time and the* GIRLS *follow behind them. Both of them are on crutches and their heads are bandaged. They too carry signs. The first* GIRL *holds one which says* AND DON'T FORGET, *and the second* GIRL *one which proclaims,* PROTECT YOURSELF.

SUGGESTIONS

This skit moves quickly. Be sure to have things ready. Of course the marchers can take up a little extra time if you need it. Maybe they could have a chant or song about ecology. In fact they could just repeat over and over in a kind of rhythmic beat "protect our meadow . . . protect our forest . . . protect our mountain." This is pantomime, but the chants pass as sound effects. After all, the marchers are somewhat like the announcers who are permitted to set the scene or fill in gaps of understanding.

Someone could be assigned to take care of the sign changes and additions. Another could whisk off the litter can. The gauze wrappings on the girls' arms could be in place in the first scene but covered with long-sleeved shirts. Band-Aids are applied in seconds. If the changes are still too difficult, you can always use different actors in each scene.

Suggest the trees by having the players hold branches. Put a nest in the hair of one or two and perhaps hang signs around their necks: SPRUCE, PINE, FIR, OAK.

The characters here could just as well be all boys, or boys and girls.

WHAT TOOK YOU SO LONG?

Characters

THE OFF-STAGE VOICE

THE SPECTATORS, AS MANY AS DESIRED

THE WOULD-BE STOWAWAY

THE TWO ASTRONAUTS

THE GUARD

THE PEOPLE ON THE PLANET, ANY NUMBER

The curtain opens on Scene One, the area where the blast-off is to take place. The left third of the stage is roped off and the SPECTATORS *are crowded behind it. There is a sign above their heads,* SPACE STATION. *The space ship is off-stage to the right.*

The SPECTATORS *look out toward the back of the auditorium. They wave various banners:* MARS, HERE WE COME . . . LET'S BE FRIENDS . . . WE GO UP, YOU COME DOWN. *The* ASTRONAUTS *approach from the rear of the room, mount the steps to the stage, nod and wave to the crowd, and exit right.*

OFF-STAGE VOICE. We've gathered here today to launch the first trip to Mars. Two of our finest astronauts take off in a matter of minutes and, just as it was with the moon venture, our men will be the first to set foot on the red planet. What they will find there, we'll soon know. Watch for complete coverage on your viewing screens . . .

The WOULD-BE STOWAWAY, *who is in the crowd, slips under the rope and approaches the* GUARD. *He whispers something to him in an excited manner. The* GUARD *shakes his head and escorts the person back to the crowd.*

OFF-STAGE VOICE. Everything seems to be going according to schedule. It won't be long now.

The STOWAWAY *slips under the rope again. This time he tries to sneak past the* GUARD *and to the right exit. He is stopped and once more put back behind the barrier. The* GUARD *is rougher with him.*

OFF-STAGE VOICE. The men are now in their seats. Everything is in order . . .

The STOWAWAY *throws a rubber ball over the heads of the crowd to distract attention from himself. There is a flurry of excitement as the people panic, thinking it is a bomb. The* GUARD *retrieves the ball, and he bounces it around to show that it is a harmless toy. While this is going on, the* STOWAWAY *ducks under the rope a third time and runs for the exit. No one notices him, and he makes it.*

OFF-STAGE VOICE. The time has come . . . 10–9–8–whoops, there's trouble . . . (*There is a pause.*)

The STOWAWAY *is shoved back onto the stage. He sits just inside the exit as the* OFF-STAGE VOICE *continues.*

OFF-STAGE VOICE. (*starts countdown again*) 10–9–8–7–6–5–4–3–2–1– (*There is a great whooshing sound.*)

The SPECTATORS *look up, watching the takeoff and following the space craft out of sight.* (*The curtain closes.*)

The ASTRONAUTS *enter in front of the closed curtain, walking as on the moon—weightless with a kind of bouncing movement. They cross back and forth a couple of times until the curtain opens.*

SCENE TWO

The stage is dimly lit. As the ASTRONAUTS *move in from the right the lights go up to reveal a group of* PEOPLE. *They are obviously celebrating some kind of an anniversary. There is a huge sign,* FIVE YEARS ON MARS, *at the left of the group, and one of the* PEOPLE *lifts another sign:* WHAT TOOK YOU SO LONG?

SUGGESTIONS

Strictly speaking, as a pantomime you might be upset about the off-stage voice. Still, the speaker is not seen and simply introduces the action and provides the background sound effects. I'm sure your audience will accept that.

The buildup before the blast-off is important and as much can be made of it as you wish. The real impact of this skit, however, comes with the discovery of the group already on the planet. This is where you tailor the punch to fit your needs. If you are using this for a Scout program, a Scout Troop (your own local one, of course) could be sitting around a campfire in the second scene. You might not even want the "five year" sign. It will be enough just that they are there. Also the would-be stowaway could be in Scout uniform. Naturally he wanted to join his troop.

If this is a school program, put on by the fifth graders perhaps, the group on Mars could be none other than the fifth graders of your school. Or you might use a women's lib idea. The astronauts are men. The group on Mars turns out to be women. In each case the would-be stowaway could be a member of the group already on the planet. The possibilities are limitless. Provide your own gimmick.

The costumes can be merely suggestive of the real thing. Coveralls or jump suits, large ones padded with towels to give bulk, also padded gloves and, of course, helmets. Space headgear is usually cylindrically shaped. Why not use commercial ice cream containers? A local ice cream shop might oblige. Good old brown paper bags are always adaptable. Or if you really want to spend time, you could make the helmets of papier-mâché.

The blast-off sound can probably be found on a record, but your audience isn't going to expect authenticity. Experiment with verbal whooshing provided by many backstage voices. If your sound is a little ridiculous or if the takeoff is a silent one, you might get a laugh—and that's something you can always use.

Incidentally, the planet doesn't have to be Mars. Maybe there is some other exciting possibility. If you do use Mars, however, why not have a glow of red in the lighting?

THE HAUNTED HOUSE

CHARACTERS

MR. SLY
THE ADVENTURER
THREE WILLING COMPANIONS
MR. WON'T GO
HEAD GHOST
OTHER GHOSTS

As the skit is announced MR. SLY *comes from the back of the auditorium or from the wings. He sets up his table at the right in front of the curtain, and on it he puts two large placards:* BIG ADVENTURE—ONLY $5 *and* GO IN—COME OUT—COLLECT THE BAG OF GOLD. MR. SLY *takes a bag filled with stones or something similar to give it weight and plunks it down. Then he goes to the center opening of the curtain and pins a third placard there,* HAUNTED HOUSE.

When he returns to the table, the ADVENTURER (*who is the leader*) *enters from the left with his four followers. They see the signs. The leader points first to the one which says* HAUNTED HOUSE, *then to the others. He asks his companions, with a gesture, if they will go in.* MR. WON'T GO *gives a negative answer and exits. The other three raise their hands in approval, and the leader collects money from them and advances to the table.* MR. SLY *accepts the fees and registers satisfaction as the four brave ones enter through the opening of the curtain.* MR. SLY *picks up a magazine and settles back to read.* (*The curtain opens on a stage set with four sheet-covered pieces of furniture. Eerie music plays and grotesque masks are spotlighted around the room.)*

The leader wends his way back and forth across the stage, his followers behind him. He goes from one to another of the sheeted objects removing the covers with a swagger of fearlessness. Each time he does this a white-shrouded GHOST *enters from offstage, picks up the discarded covering, and uses it to envelop the last person in line. He guides him off without the leader being aware of it. Finally there is only the leader left. He unveils the last chair, but, as he turns to tell his companions they can leave now, he is also confronted with a* GHOST*—the* HEAD GHOST*—and is led away as the curtain closes.*

Attention is directed again to MR. SLY. *He has stopped reading and is apparently working on another placard. The* HEAD GHOST *slips out through the center opening of the curtain. He comes to the table and puts out his hand to receive his share of the money.* MR. SLY *rejects his demand and sends him off.*

Finally SLY *finishes his sign, counts his money, and goes to the center of the stage where the* HAUNTED HOUSE *placard still hangs. He puts his new sign beside it,* 1111, *and is about to leave when sheeted arms reach out and pull him through the opening. Then the* HEAD GHOST *emerges and marks the tally:* ~~1111~~. *The eerie music gets louder and chains rattle as the ghost goes back inside.*

Suggestions

Mr. Sly is the villain of this skit, a sly one as his name indicates. He might be dressed with that in mind—dark clothes and a top hat perhaps, with a black mustache and eyebrows to match. Or he could appear as a ruffian with a cap drawn down over his eyes. The magazine he reads could be a ghost comic book with pictures on the cover large enough to be seen.

The customers might be just the people as they are, recognizable to the audience.

The ghosts need only sheets, of course, and the eerie setting can be as elaborate as you wish to make it. If it isn't possible to have spotlights, the adventurers could carry flashlights. As a Halloween skit, all the rattling chains and background sounds you can provide will add to the effect.

If you want to cut down on characters, only one ghost is necessary.

YOU CAN'T WIN 'EM ALL

CHARACTERS

THE PROPRIETOR
THE MAN
THE WOMAN } THE TRAVELERS
THE CHILD

Scene One is laid at THE DOG AND DONUT, *a wayside snack shop in an out-of-the-way section of the country. It's the kind of place which opens for business by lifting up the top front section to disclose the counter. There are stools for the customers and a large standing sign at the left which announces* THE DOG AND DONUT. *Curtain opens.*

The PROPRIETOR *who is behind the counter is young and brisk. He has a towel wrapped around his waist and a chef's cap on his head. He winds the big alarm clock which sits on one end of the counter and which indicates that it is noon. He dusts off a placard menu and sets it up in full view of the audience. He is polishing a glass when there is the sound of a car. He puts down the glass and comes out of the shop to greet the* TRAVELERS.

The MAN *enters from the left, pulls a map from his pocket, and strides over to the* PROPRIETOR. *The* WOMAN *enters. She is smiling and moves with a quick step. The* LITTLE GIRL *skips in behind her.*

The PROPRIETOR *ignores the man when he sees the others and moves over to the counter indicating items on the menu—hot dogs, French fries, doughnuts. The* WOMAN *gives a negative gesture suggesting she is too heavy, but the* LITTLE GIRL *hops up on one of the stools.*

The MAN, *however, waves the menu aside, spreads his map out on the counter, and bends over it obviously asking directions. The* PROPRIETOR *is disappointed, but he looks at the map. Then he straightens up and gives directions which are quite involved. The* MAN *motions the* WOMAN *and* CHILD *to follow him, and they exit left.*

The PROPRIETOR *glances at his watch, shakes his head, and goes back into his shop. (Curtain closes.)*

SCENE TWO

(The curtain opens almost at once. The alarm clock now indicates five o'clock.)

The PROPRIETOR, *who is leaning on the counter, picks up the clock, looks at it, and puts it out of sight. He removes his chef's hat and the towel. Then he comes out of the shop and pulls down the section that closes things up. This reveals a fancy sign which says* RED CARPET CAFE. *Underneath this he hangs a banner declaring* HOME COOKING. *He takes away the* DOG AND DONUT *sign and brings out a small sidewalk table and a couple of chairs. Finally he rolls out a little red carpet.*

When this is all finished he sits down at the table, puts on a mustache, and pats a little powder on his temples to gray them. At last he dons a coat and tie and assumes the role of head waiter. There is the sound of a car, and the PROPRIETOR *prepares to greet the* TRAVELERS *again.*

The same MAN, WOMAN, *and* CHILD *enter, this time from the right. They look a little weary and their steps are slower. The* LITTLE GIRL *points to the restaurant sign and indicates she's hungry. She goes over to the table and gets ready to eat, but the* MAN *pulls out his map and lays it on the table. He points to his watch suggesting he doesn't have much time. The* PROPRIETOR *looks annoyed, tries to get them into the restaurant, but finally looks down at the map. He gives directions again, different ones. Then the* MAN *exits. The* LITTLE GIRL *hangs back and starts to cry. The* WOMAN *takes her by the hand and they follow the man off to the right.* (*Curtain.*)

SCENE THREE

(*The curtain opens almost at once. It is getting dark and the stage lights are dimmed.*)

The PROPRIETOR *is rolling up the carpet. He takes down the restaurant signs and removes the table and chairs. Then he puts up a new sign:* PRAIRIE MOTEL—COZY CABINS. *He exchanges his coat and tie for a sweater, brings out a rocker, and dusts his hair with powder, making it quite white. There is the sound of a car, but this time the* PROPRIETOR *just sits and rocks with a smile on his face.*

The TRAVELERS *enter from the left. This time the* MAN *is carrying suitcases. The* WOMAN *is dragging the* CHILD *by the hand. They are bedraggled and exhausted. They come over to the rocker, but the old fellow pretends he can't hear. He seems reluctant to get up, but when they indicate with motions that they want a cabin, he finally rises slowly and points to the rear. The* MAN *pulls out his wallet just as the* CHILD, *who has brightened up and is poking around, pulls out the* DOG AND DONUT *sign. The* MAN *glances over at it perplexed. The* CHILD *then discovers the* RED CARPET *sign and the* HOME COOKING *one. It dawns on all the travelers what has happened. The* MAN *puts back his money and, motioning to his family to follow him, walks off in anger. The* WOMAN *frowns and the* LITTLE GIRL *makes a face at the old codger, and they exit.*

The proprietor turns to the audience with an impish grin. He shrugs as the curtain closes.

SUGGESTIONS

The players have a chance to do a bit of acting here. The travelers can get more tired and disheveled with each appearance. The proprietor not only changes his clothes and adds facial make-up, but is transformed from a quick-stepping young fellow to an old timer. Of course, he is really young. Remember to have him move briskly during the changes and right up to the time he assumes his role of the moment. Incidentally, since the proprietor sets the stage, you don't have to worry about allowing time between scenes.

The props shouldn't be too difficult. The signs, the stools, the table and chairs, the rocker should all be easy to acquire. If you can come up with some kind of counter for the first scene—and why couldn't you work something out with that old standby, the refrigerator carton—you're all set.

If you can't find some way of providing the sound of the car and brakes (on a record perhaps) you can always use just a horn.

Costumes are dictated by the roles, and of course don't forget the suitcases in Scene Three.

QUICK! THE RIVER'S RISING

CHARACTERS

THE MAN IN AUTHORITY, OFF-STAGE VOICE
THE WOMAN WITH THE CLOTHES
THE CHILD WITH THE BLANKET
THE BOY WITH THE BICYCLE
THE GIRL WITH THE BALLOONS
THE CHILD WITH THE STUFFED ANIMAL
THE WOMAN WITH THE PILLOWS
THE BOY WITH THE FOOD

The scene is the main street of the town. When the curtain opens, a loudspeaker from offstage blares out instructions.

OFF-STAGE VOICE. Attention! The river is rising. There is a real threat to the Downer Flats area. You may have no more than thirty minutes to get to safety. Everyone on the south bank from Jefferson to Military Avenue, *move.* I repeat . . . *Move!* Take only what you can carry and leave. Time is running out.

(As the message is repeated at three- or four-second intervals the townspeople enter from the right and exit left.)

The first person to flee is a BOY *with a large and obviously heavy brown paper bag. It contains food—sandwiches, cookies, fruit. He stops every step or two and eats, sometimes sitting down. The others come on stage, pass him by, and exit.*

A WOMAN *enters burdened with extra clothing. She has three or four coats on and several hats piled up on her head. Over her arm there are four or five handbags, and she carries two or three suitcases with clothing hanging out. She drops a handbag, stoops to pick it up, loses the hats. Finally she manages to get off left, but the hats are squashed and everything is in a muddle. She clutches one purse under her chin and kicks a couple of hats along as she moves.*

A CHILD *enters carrying a blanket. He chews on one corner while the rest of it trails behind him.*

A BOY *enters carrying his bicycle. Apparently it doesn't occur to him to ride it to safety.*

One little GIRL *has an armload of balloons. As she moves across the stage, they get away from her one by one. She finds herself with a single balloon which pops just as she exits.*

One CHILD *tugs at a long rope as though with great effort. It isn't until he reaches the left exit that his prize possession emerges—a stuffed animal, a dog perhaps.*

A WOMAN *carries a couple of large bed pillows.*

The skit ends with the BOY *who has eaten his food. When he looks in the empty sack he blows it up and pops it. Then he turns to the audience and shrugs as he goes off.*

SUGGESTIONS

If you have a curtain, close it quickly at the end. Otherwise you might have the off-stage voice still repeating the message and perhaps have someone come in to announce the skit's end—even to the point of telling the voice "Be quiet."

Any number of characters can escape the flood, and it might be fun to put in some people known to your group. This is a time when your actors can change costumes and come on again. Obviously, they don't have to learn any lines. Just don't let it become too long or monotonous so that the punch action is ineffective.

SUNDAY AT MEADOWLAKE MANOR

CHARACTERS

THE HOSTESS

RESIDENTS OF THE HOME, FIVE OR SIX OR AS MANY AS DESIRED

THE NURSE, IN WHITE UNIFORM

THE VISITORS, FRIENDS, AND RELATIVES OF RESIDENTS

The scene is the parlor at Meadowlake Manor, a retirement residence for elderly people. It is Sunday, Visitor's Day. There are as many chairs as necessary to accommodate the residents and a number of expected guests. There is a table at the center rear and on it a small radio. As the curtain opens there is soft music playing . . . old tunes . . . and the RESIDENTS *are seated around the room. One rocks monotonously, drumming her fingers on the rocker arm. A couple of old men sit idly at the table. Another just sits twiddling his thumbs. One old woman knits and another dozes, emitting an occasional snore.*

The HOSTESS *bustles in from the right bringing a vase of flowers and a game of checkers. She puts the flowers on the table and sets up the game for the old men. Then she moves one of the empty chairs up to one group and adjusts the radio so that it can barely be heard.*

The NURSE *enters from the right. She fluffs up a pillow at the back of one little old lady and hands a large picture book to another. She wakes (or tries to) the dozing woman, pats her arm, and whispers something to her.*

From offstage a clock is heard to strike two. The HOSTESS *exits left and in a moment returns with* VISITORS—*the friends, children, and grandchildren of the residents. They all hurry to their respective relatives, and there is the pantomime of admiration for the knitting of the one, the necklace of another. Someone watches the checker game for a few minutes. The lady who is visiting the sleeper shakes her arm, tries to chat with her, finally gives up and just sits there beside her.*

The old people smile and nod in a bored, blank way and do everything that is expected of them.

Finally the guests leave, escorted out by the HOSTESS *and followed by the* NURSE. *There is complete silence and no movement for a moment. Then the woman who had been rocking gets up and walks with a sprightly step to the exit and peers offstage. When she turns around she nods her head with a broad smile, and the whole scene changes.*

*The knitter puts aside her yarn and pulls a current magazine from her knitting bag—*True Confessions, *perhaps, or a very modern periodical geared to "the new woman." The men put away the checkers and tune in some up-to-date music on the radio, something with a young fast beat. And the woman who was sleeping gives one loud snore, wakes up, responds to the music, and dances with youthful enthusiasm as the curtain falls.*

SUGGESTIONS

This is a skit which requires little in the way of staging and adapts easily to an all-boy or all-girl cast. Instead of the hostess, there could be a doctor. Give the player a toy stethoscope around the neck, and if a boy is playing the part, add a mustache. A male nurse could wear a white coat.

There is also an opportunity to add characters that might have identity for the audience. In fact the skit could be set in a future year and the residents of Meadowlake Manor be the parents of the performers or the faculty and principal of the school. It could poke light-hearted fun at the adults and then end with a tribute to their youthful outlook.

Make the characters old by all the usual means: powdered hair, canes, hearing trumpets, shawls, and "sensible shoes." The older they are in appearance and action at the beginning the more effective the transformation.

HIBERNIAN PICNIC

Characters

THE IRISH, AS MANY AS YOU WISH

SMITH, THE OUTSIDER

As the curtain opens, the KELLYS, *the* O'HOULIHANS, *the* O'BRIENS, *and the* O'NEALS *all enter from the right. They wear enormous buttons and carry standards which bear their names. Some of them carry picnic baskets, blankets, radios.*

Someone takes the center of the stage to dance a jig; someone else mouths an Irish song to music played off-stage. One group huddles in silent laughter over a story that has been told.

SMITH, *the stranger, comes in from the left. He has a standard bearing his name, and he strides in with confidence, eager to join the fun. When he is noticed, he is ejected from the scene. He comes back with an "O" in front of his name. His placard now reads* O'SMITH, *and he mingles a bit until someone takes a good look at him and his sign. Once more he is ousted, more forcefully this time, maybe even bodily to add to the action.*

Completely discouraged, SMITH *sneaks back to the edge of the festive group. He watches sadly; then he hits upon a new idea. He runs from the stage and returns with an American flag which he affixes to his standard and proudly circles the crowd, marching round and round with great dignity.*

Someone comes to send him away again, but he points to the flag and the bouncer withdraws and reports to the leader of the picnickers. There is a flurry of excitement and a huddled conference. A decision is made, and the stranger is jubilantly welcomed to the party while a new banner is raised: THE AMERICAN WAY.

SUGGESTIONS

No scenery is needed here, and the pantomime could be performed anywhere, even without a stage.

The placards are essential, but are easily made from cardboard. All the other props can be as elaborate or as simple as you wish—anything to provide a picnic or festival atmosphere.

The Irish should wear a great deal of green in contrast to Smith. Certainly oversize shamrocks should be displayed on their lapels, hats, or armbands.

Of course the whole idea could be reversed. In an area where another nationality or race predominates, the Irishman could be a loner with no one to celebrate with him. At the end he welcomes the crowd.

NONE BUT THE STRONG

CHARACTERS

GRANDMA

THE CHILDREN

*The curtain rises on a very simple set. There is a big sign at the left—*GIANT DIP ROLLER COASTER*—and another on the right—*RIDE AT YOUR OWN RISK. *At the center of the stage is a row of seats arranged to suggest a coaster car.*

Several children enter, herded along by a little old lady. The CHILDREN *jump up and down and point to the signs.* GRANDMA *tries to hold them back, shakes her head "no," and expresses fear. They plead with her, and one child even gets on his knees. Finally she is pulled unwillingly to the car.*

When they are seated, the mechanism starts up, and the audience can see by the swaying backwards that the roller coaster is starting its climb. With facial expressions to match the excitement, the ride progresses. The CHILDREN *mouth their shouts of glee and anticipation, and* GRANDMA *hangs on in terror.*

They sway forward, down the dip, and as they go up again it is the CHILDREN *who become frightened.* GRANDMA *begins to enjoy herself, and we see her relax and smile. One child covers his face. Another gets down on the floor. Another just screams (without sound of course), and when they get back to the starting point, they all crawl out on unsteady legs, glad to get off. All except* GRANDMA. *She refuses to budge, and the* CHILDREN *watch with open mouths as she settles in for the next ride and the coaster starts once more.* (*Curtain.*)

SUGGESTIONS

This pantomime could very easily be performed without a stage. Facial expression and exaggerated action are actually what put it over. You can see, however, that a quick curtain at the end would be more effective.

The old lady can be as old as you care to make her. A cane, a shawl, an old-fashioned handbag will all add character. Actually she's probably a great-grandmother.

The children are just children, and it is always a good idea to make them younger than the actors who portray them.

If you wish you can add another character by having an attendant who takes up the tickets. Or better yet, have him sell the tickets to the group as well.

PART III

THE PUPPET PLAY

THE PUPPET PLAY

. . . a show of hands . . .

The puppet show, like the pantomime, reaches back to ancient times for its beginnings. The idea of dolls performing as though they are alive holds a special appeal.

If you have begun your play-acting with pantomime where you had no lines to learn, the next step might be the puppet show. Many of the lines can be given to a narrator, and the puppeteers need to speak only as much as you wish them to. This is especially important if there is a problem of being heard from below and behind the stage opening.

Of the puppet plays in this book, *Tillie's Terror* is the easiest to perform. The characters scream and laugh and sing, but otherwise say very little. The narrator carries the story. Some of the other plays are more complicated, but they could be changed if necessary. You might want to use them all, moving from the simplest to the most difficult.

All in favor—hands up.

WOMEN'S LIB COMES TO THE HILL COUNTRY

CHARACTERS

ANNOUNCER, NOT A PUPPET

PA CRACKER

MS. CRACKER

JUDY MAE, THEIR DAUGHTER

The curtain of the puppet theater is closed as the announcer speaks to the audience.

ANNOUNCER. All the tales you've ever heard about the old mountain people tell of the laziness of the menfolk. And all the pictures you see show the women and girls dragging around doing the chores while the men and boys just sit or sleep in the sun. Well, we always felt sure that if the women were given half a chance they'd wipe out that kind of injustice, and if they really put their minds to it they could excel at everything . . . even at being lazy. Let's look in on a little post-liberation scene deep in the hill country.

(*The curtain of the puppet theater opens to reveal the interior of a mountain cabin.* MS. CRACKER *sits leaning against the right wall and* JUDY MAE *sits leaning against the left. There is a backdrop which shows a window, and* PA *is sitting at the left side of it.*)

ANNOUNCER. That's Pa Cracker over there by the window. He's asleep all right.

PA CRACKER. (*snores*)

ANNOUNCER. There's Ms. Cracker over there on the right, and the other one's Judy Mae, their daughter. Listen now.

JUDY MAE. Where's pa?

MS. CRACKER. He's settin' over there. Can't ya hear him?

PA CRACKER. (*snores*)

JUDY MAE. Oh, I can hear him, but I can't see him less I turn my head. Too tired to do that.

MS. CRACKER. It don't matter. He ain't doin' nothin'.

JUDY MAE. Got any more corn chips left, ma?

MS. CRACKER. (*turns the sack upside down*) Nope.

JUDY MAE. I'm sure gettin' hungry, ma.

MS. CRACKER. Me too.

JUDY MAE. You gonna fix supper, ma?

MS. CRACKER. I ain't that hungry.

PA CRACKER. (*snores*)

JUDY MAE. Hey, ma! I smell smoke. (*She sniffs.*)

MS. CRACKER. (*sniffs*) Me too. You smell that smoke, pa?

PA CRACKER. (*snores*)

JUDY MAE. I think the cabin's burnin', ma.

MS. CRACKER. Must be. Pa ain't smokin'.

JUDY MAE. You gonna put out the fire, ma?

MS. CRACKER. Don't see why. I didn't start it.

JUDY MAE. It's gettin' hot in here, ma.

MS. CRACKER. You can say that again, girl.

JUDY MAE. It's gettin' terrible hot in here, ma.

PA CRACKER. (*snores again and wakes up*) Hey, ma. The cabin's burnin'.

MS. CRACKER. We know it, pa.

PA CRACKER. Ain't you two gonna get out of here? (*coughs*)

MS. CRACKER. I just ain't hankerin' to move, pa. (*coughs*)

JUDY MAE. Me neither. (*coughs*)

PA CRACKER. Well, I'm agoin'. It's too hot for me. (*He exits.*)

MS. CRACKER. (*calls after him*) Guess you got more energy than us, pa.

(MS. CRACKER *and* JUDY MAE *cough and sputter.* PA CRACKER *appears at the window and leans in.*)

PA CRACKER. The roof's gonna cave in any minute.

JUDY MAE. It sure is. (*looking up*)

MS. CRACKER. Looks like this is the end, Judy Mae.

JUDY MAE. Looks like, ma.

MS. CRACKER. W-elll, one thing. I'm sure glad I didn't waste no time fixin' supper. (*They cough and make choking sounds as the roof caves in and the curtain closes.*)

SUGGESTIONS

It would be very appropriate if the announcer were a women's libber. She could parade in carrying a RIGHT ON sign and address the audience as though it was one of her speaking tour stops.

The puppets will be fun to costume. Long black whiskers and a black hat for pa, braids for Judy Mae, and loose, scraggly hair tied back with a string for Ms. Cracker.

I suppose you could make a little corn chip sack and fasten it to Ms. Cracker's hand. She can shake it at the proper time without even having to let go of it. And that's about the only prop required.

The dialogue will carry the show. You don't need to provide smoke and fire, but the roof can certainly cave in. A pull of a string can release sticks and stones and pieces of cardboard which have been poised above the puppet stage.

FLAT, FLAT, FLAT

CHARACTERS

THE NARRATOR, NOT A PUPPET
THE KING
THE SULTAN
THE DICTATOR
THE TYRANT, THE SUPER SOVEREIGN OF SAMOO
THE PEASANT
THE CHIEF ADVISOR
CITIZEN ONE
CITIZEN TWO
THE GUARD
BOY, THE TYRANT'S SON

The narrator enters and stands at the side of the puppet theater as its curtain opens. There is a backdrop scene of a castle with a window in the center near the top.

NARRATOR. Once upon a time there was a king. (*Puppet* KING *enters from the left.*) Well, I think he was a king. Maybe he was a sultan. (SULTAN *enters left and tries to push the* KING *off the stage.*) But then again, I'm not sure. Possibly he was a dictator. (*Puppet* DICTATOR *enters left and the three start to fight.* NARRATOR *listens to someone in the audience.*) No . . . no. It wasn't . . . it couldn't have been a president . . . certainly not our president . . . no way. (*The fighting among the rulers gets noisy and the* NARRATOR *turns toward them.*) Stop that, all of you. As a matter of fact, I remember now. It wasn't any of you. Go on, get along and squabble someplace else. (*They exit and the* NARRATOR *speaks to the audience again.*) Actually it wasn't a king, or a sultan, or a dictator. It was really something else. It was a terrible tyrant, and he had absolute power over his subjects. They did exactly what he told them to do. (TYRANT *enters left.*) There, I think we've got the right one now . . . listen . . .

TYRANT. (*shouts to someone offstage*) You . . . You out there. Come here at once.

(*The* PEASANT *enters and bows low.*)

TYRANT. I want you to tie my shoe.

PEASANT. (*looks down and of course sees no shoes . . . or feet, for that matter, since these are hand puppets*) But I can't, your mighty majesty.

TYRANT. Don't be impudent. Do as I say.

PEASANT. But your mighty majesty. It is impossible. Where are your shoes?

TYRANT. Where do you think they are? On my feet, of course.

PEASANT. But your mighty majesty, I see no shoes. I don't even see your feet.

TYRANT. No excuse. No excuse at all. Guard. Guard. (GUARD *enters.*) Take this impertinent fellow to the dungeon. When I say a thing is to be done, it is to be done.

(GUARD *exits with the* PEASANT *who covers his eyes with his hands and moans. The* TYRANT *remains on the stage, pacing back and forth.*)

NARRATOR. That was a hard command, you know. I can't see his feet either. Can you? Well, this was a pretty bad situation, all right, but it got worse. The terrible tyrant decided his subjects should not only do what he told them to do, they must believe what he told them to believe. And that kind of thing can lead to real trouble. You know it. Especially when one of the things he commanded them to believe was . . . well, just listen . . .

TYRANT. (*shouts to someone offstage*) Send in my chief advisor. (CHIEF ADVISOR *enters.*) I wish to give out an edict. (*He coughs and clears his throat.*)

ADVISOR. Yes, your mighty majesty.

TYRANT. I want you to post an announcement on all the bulletin boards in the country: THE WORLD IS FLAT. Throw out all the books that say it is not.

ADVISOR. But the world isn't flat, your mighty majesty.

TYRANT. Don't contradict me. I am the super sovereign of Samoo. If I say the world is flat, it's flat. Guard. (GUARD *enters.*) Take my chief advisor to the dungeon. (*The* GUARD *exits left with the* ADVISOR *and the* TYRANT *exits right.*)

NARRATOR. Well, the terrible tyrant posted the bulletin himself and threw out the books, but the citizens of Samoo were very confused. (CITIZENS ONE *and* TWO *enter from the right.*)

CITIZEN ONE. I'm confused. Have you seen the latest edict?

CITIZEN TWO. He's got to be kidding.

CITIZEN ONE. We all know that the world is round . . . don't we?

CITIZEN TWO. Of course we do. Pretty soon he'll be having us living in caves . . .

NARRATOR. Some of the citizens even dared to laugh. (CITIZENS *laugh.*) But word got around to the terrible tyrant and he was furious.

TYRANT. (*appears at the window of the castle*) I am furious. How dare you contradict me down there. The world is flat, flat, flat, and you will believe it.

CITIZENS. We won't believe it, because it isn't true.

NARRATOR. You notice they no longer call him mighty majesty.

TYRANT. Guard! Guard! (*No one appears.*)

NARRATOR. Well, the tyrant shouted for his guard, but no one came and he had to come down out of his castle and take the citizens to the dungeon himself. (*The* TYRANT *comes down and pushes the* CITIZENS *off.*) It wasn't long before half of Samoo was in the dungeon and the other half was in a difficult position. They didn't believe the world was flat, but they didn't believe in dungeons either. It was quite a problem. Then one day the tyrant was in the garden talking to his son. He didn't care much for children, but there weren't many people around anymore for him to talk to. (TYRANT *enters with the* BOY.)

TYRANT. You believe what I say, don't you, boy. The world is flat.

BOY. No, I don't, father. I read about the round world before you threw out the books. And I believe the books.

TYRANT. Oh, I was too late. I don't see how I can put my own son in the dungeon. I'll just have to prove to you that I am right. (*They exit as the curtain closes.*)

NARRATOR. The tyrant took his son on a long journey. They traveled for days and days until finally . . .

(*Curtain opens and the* TYRANT *and the* BOY *enter left. The scene has been changed. The castle back-*

drop is gone and there is a sign about the middle of the stage: END OF THE WORLD. DON'T GO BEYOND THIS POINT.)

BOY. You see, father, we haven't come to the edge of the world.

TYRANT. Well, there it is. Right up ahead there. Don't you see the sign? I put it up myself.

BOY. A sign doesn't make it so. Did you ever go up to find out?

TYRANT. Certainly not. If I were to take one step beyond that sign, I would fall over the side. Can't you understand that?

BOY. That is ridiculous, father. The world is round. There is only a little dip in the meadow up there.

TYRANT. Oh, that I should have such a son. I will show you how wrong you are. (*He goes one step beyond the sign and drops down catching himself with his hands on the edge of the stage. All the audience can see are his hands.*) You see, you see. I have fallen off the edge of the world. Save me.

BOY. It is all in your mind, father. I'll show you. He walks to the same place and remains upright.

TYRANT. (*still clutching the edge of the stage*) Help me! Help me! I am the super sovereign of Samoo. Save me! I can't hold on much longer . . .

BOY. But father, if you believe such a foolish thing I can't help you. You shall probably drop into space. You will vanish. You will be no more. (*He exits and the* TYRANT *loses his grip and falls with a cry as the curtain closes.*)

NARRATOR. The story has rather a happy ending though. The tyrant's son didn't want to be super sovereign of Samoo or anybody's mighty majesty. The citizens decided to have a democracy. They let everybody out of the dungeons and elected a president. The boy, of course, missed his father and he posted a big sign replacing the one at the dip in the meadow. (*Curtain opens and the* BOY *puts up a sign:* BE VERY CAREFUL ABOUT WHAT YOU BELIEVE. *The* NARRATOR *exits as the curtain closes.*)

SUGGESTIONS

Each puppet needs only one or two identifying bits of costume. The king, a crown and purple robe. The sultan, a turban. The dictator, a beard—or why not a Hitler-like mustache. The tyrant might be a combination of the other three with a purple robe, a turban, and the dictator's beard or mustache.

The peasant might have a stocking cap on his head, and the guard a high, plumed headdress. The citizens' hair could be full and free-flowing, and why not have a bald advisor with ribbons and medals around his neck. Give the boy a small crown and then have it be removed for the last scene.

If you don't want to involve as many puppets as called for, you could eliminate the first scene and begin with the tyrant. You could also do without the castle backdrop, but it adds a little variety to have the ruler appear at the window.

BEWARE OF THE GLUMP

CHARACTERS

THE NARRATOR, NOT A PUPPET

THE CHILDREN OF THE TOWN, AS MANY AS YOU WISH

THE WOMAN OF THE TOWN, WITH AN ENORMOUS NOSE

THE MAN OF THE TOWN, WITH HUGE FLOPPY EARS

THE MAYOR OF THE TOWN, WITH THICK SHAGGY EYEBROWS

THE STRANGER

C. Q. GLUMP, ESQUIRE

The NARRATOR *comes out to stand at the side of the puppet theater and speaks to the audience.*

NARRATOR. Once upon a time there was a town called Sidnitz. And there in the town, down by the river road, there lived a man named Glump. C. Q. Glump. At least I'm quite sure he lived there. No one ever went to see him. You see, everyone was afraid of the glump. That's what they called him . . . the glump. Certainly all the children had strict instructions to stay away from the river road. In fact, they used to chant the warning all the way to school in the morning.

(*Curtain opens on a street in the town. There is a backdrop of buildings and at the left end there is a sign:* THE MAYOR. *Attached to the sign is a little bell. The* CHILDREN *enter right and go across the stage chanting, "Stay away from the river road . . . stay away from the river road." They exit left.)*

NARRATOR. And all the way home. (CHILDREN *enter left and go back across the stage chanting, "The glump, the glump . . . Beware of the glump." They exit right as the* NARRATOR *continues.*) No one ever knew why the people were afraid. No one ever talked about it. Then one day a stranger came to town. He had business with C. Q. Glump, and he started to inquire around . . . well, just listen . . .

(*The* STRANGER *enters from the right. He wears a long coat and a black drooping-brimmed hat. The* WOMAN *of the town enters from the left and they meet.*)

STRANGER. Good morning, madam. Can you tell me where I will find a Mr. Glump?

WOMAN. *Who* did you say?

STRANGER. Mr. Glump, madam. C. Q. Glump. I have business with him.

WOMAN. Oh dear me, I was afraid you'd said glump. I tell you, stranger, they say the glump lives down by the river road, but I shouldn't go there if I were you.

STRANGER. And why shouldn't I?

WOMAN. The glump is a terrible creature. (*She comes close to the* STRANGER *and whispers.*) I've only seen him once and that was enough. He has this enormous nose . . . Oh dear, I've talked too much already. You'll have to excuse me. (*She exits left.*)

STRANGER. (*calls after her*) But madam, you have . . . (*He realizes she is out of earshot. He turns and mumbles to himself.*) Enormous nose, indeed. I'll just have to ask someone else. (*He moves slowly toward the exit right.*)

NARRATOR. Well, the stranger was a little perplexed, but just then a man of the town came along the street. (MAN *enters right.*)

MAN. You seem to be a stranger, mister. Can I do something for you?

STRANGER. Perhaps you can, sir. Which way do I go to get to the river road?

MAN. The river road!

STRANGER. Yes. I understand Mr. Glump lives down that way. I have business with him.

MAN. With the glump? What possible business could you have with the glump?

STRANGER. That's my business, sir. Can you direct me?

MAN. I wouldn't direct my worst enemy to the river road, mister. The glump is a frightful creature.

STRANGER. But why is he so frightful? An enormous nose is nothing to be afraid of.

MAN. Oh, it's not his nose, mister. It's his . . . (*he hesitates*) Well, I might as well tell you, although I've not spoken of it to a living soul. He has these huge floppy ears . . . frightful, mister, frightful. No, I wouldn't direct you, mister. Forget it. Just forget it. (*He scurries off to the right leaving the* STRANGER *calling after him.*)

STRANGER. But come back, sir. Don't you know that . . .

NARRATOR. Well, the stranger was getting a little impatient. Then he noticed that right there on the street was the office of the mayor of the town. He went up and rang the little bell which hung above the door. (*The* STRANGER *has moved to the left end of the street. He rings the bell, and the* MAYOR *emerges.*)

STRANGER. Your honor, you are the mayor of Sidnitz?

MAYOR. I am indeed. What can I do for you, stranger?

STRANGER. I have been trying to get directions to the river road. I want to see Mr. Glump.

MAYOR. Well, now that's an unfortunate request, stranger.

STRANGER. But why? I have business with Mr. Glump. Won't you tell me how to get to his house?

MAYOR. Couldn't do it, stranger . . . just couldn't do it. As mayor of the town, I must think of its reputation. If I told you the way to the river road, you might . . . no, no, I'm afraid I couldn't direct you to the glump.

STRANGER. I know everyone seems to think he is a terrible, frightful creature. But I'm not afraid of an enormous nose and floppy ears. That's foolish.

MAYOR. What do you mean . . . *nose* and *ears?* If I were to tell you . . . yes, I can see you're a stubborn fellow. Come closer. (*He pulls the* STRANGER *to him and talks in an urgent voice.*) The glump is indeed a dreadful creature. It's his eyebrows . . . his thick shaggy eyebrows.

STRANGER. But your honor . . .

MAYOR. (*interrupting*) That's all I will say, and don't you tell anyone I discussed this with you, or I might not win the election next week. (MAYOR *looks to the right and left before he exits the way he came.*)

STRANGER. (*to himself*) There are certainly strange people in this town. Well, I'm not afraid of shaggy eyebrows either. I'll just find the river road by myself. (*He exits left as the curtain closes.*)

NARRATOR. The stranger was indeed baffled, but he was determined to find Mr. Glump. He walked on past the post office and the library and down beyond the cemetery to the river road. There ahead of him he saw Glump's gate.

(*Curtain opens and the* STRANGER *enters from the right. At the far left is a white picket fence with a sign on it:* C. Q. GLUMP, ESQUIRE.)

STRANGER. (*goes to the gate and calls out*) Sir! Mr. Glump, sir. I would like to talk to you.

MR. GLUMP. (*offstage*) To me! No one ever talks to me. I'll be right there.

(MR. GLUMP *enters from the left. He has an enormous nose, huge floppy ears, thick shaggy eyebrows, and a shock of red hair which stands straight up in the air.*)

MR. GLUMP. I am delighted, simply delighted. What can I do for you, sir? (*The* STRANGER *gives a great yelp and runs off right, leaving* MR. GLUMP *shaking his head in bewilderment.*) Now what in the world is the matter with him? (*Quick curtain.*)

NARRATOR. Well, the stranger made his way back to town. Past the cemetery, past the library, past the post office. And there on the main street he bumped right into the mayor who is talking to the man and the woman of the town.

WOMAN. I see you found out the glump *is* terrible with an enormous nose. I told you.

MAN. You wouldn't listen when I warned you of his huge floppy ears. Frightful.

MAYOR. Dreadful. With his . . . (*The* MAYOR *starts to say "with his thick shaggy eyebrows" and then he stops himself.*)

STRANGER. Oh, those things didn't bother me at all. What bothered me was his hair. Horrible. Horrible. I think I may faint. (*The* STRANGER *takes off his black drooping hat to fan himself and reveals a great shock of red hair which stands straight up in the air.*)

(*Quick curtain.*)

NARRATOR. (*Calls the* PUPPETEERS *out for introductions. When he has finished, he has a final word.*) Funny thing. No one ever did find out what the stranger's business was.

SUGGESTIONS

You could do without the backdrop, but it will add to the show. You might even have a door in it through which the mayor could enter.

The particular features of each puppet are called for in the script. Just remember to exaggerate the nose of the woman, the ears of the man, the brows of the mayor, and the shock of red hair on both Mr. Glump and the stranger. It must be obvious to the audience that each person fears the very feature he himself has.

WHAT COUNTS AT THE COUNTY FAIR

Characters

HENRY, THE KNOW-IT-ALL COUNTRY BUMPKIN

ZEKE, HIS SLOW-MOVING FRIEND

ELLIE, THE HEAD OF THE ASKING COMMITTEE

As the curtain opens, HENRY *hurries in from the left and crosses to the right, shouting breathlessly.*

HENRY. Zeke . . . Zeke . . . come on back here . . .

ZEKE. (*from offstage*) What's on your mind?

HENRY. Come here and I'll tell ya. (*Motions* ZEKE *to come and moves to the center of the stage as* ZEKE *enters slowly.*)

ZEKE. Well?

HENRY. (*still out of breath*) Let me get my breath a minute. I ran all the way from town.

ZEKE. Sure must be important.

HENRY. Well, I just found out they're gonna ask me to judge the beauty contest at the fair. How about that?

ZEKE. Who says?

HENRY. A very reliable source.

ZEKE. I don't want to play any guessing games . . . Who?

HENRY. Toodie! . . . Toodie Bushmiller, that's who.

ZEKE. Toodie! Forget it. She wouldn't know a truth from a tooth.

HENRY. You're just jealous, Zeke.

ZEKE. Still say I don't believe it.

HENRY. (*looks off to the left*) Well, here comes Ellie Mason now, headin' up this way. She's chairman of the askin' committee. Wait and see.

ZEKE. I'm waitin'. (*He leans up against the side of the stage.*)

HENRY. Watch me hold out on her a bit. No need to seem anxious.

(ELLIE *enters from the left*)

ELLIE. Mornin' Henry . . . Zeke. I suppose my mission has been travelin' ahead of me. 'Round fair time folks don't keep secrets.

HENRY. Reckon they don't. What you got in the bag?

ELLIE. Doughnuts. Have one, Henry.

HENRY. (*takes a doughnut*) Not bad, Ellie.

ELLIE. Fresh too. Just got 'em at the baker's not ten minutes ago . . . Now don't you get me off the point, Henry.

HENRY. Reckon I do know what you're gonna ask, Ellie, but I can't say I been givin' it much thought.

ELLIE. I ain't gonna have to coax, am I? It's a honor, and besides . . .

HENRY. I know, Ellie, but my back ain't so good lately, and I'm mighty busy this time of the year. Thanks for the doughnut.

ELLIE. How about you, Zeke? Doughnut?

ZEKE. (*moves over slowly and helps himself*) Thought you'd never ask. Don't mind if I do.

ELLIE. Now Henry, you're no busier than other folks. And we got to have competent judges. Not everybody knows good breeding.

HENRY. Well, good breeding's important all right, but I put more stock in shape myself. Weight in the right places and a proper curve or two.

ELLIE. I won't argue with you, Henry. I guess men are just better at that kind of judgin'.

HENRY. Don't want to brag, Ellie, but nobody's questioned my eye. . . . Right Zeke?

ZEKE. That's what you keep tellin' me.

HENRY. (*turns back to* ELLIE) Of course ya got to do a bit of measurin', and it takes a pat or a pinch or two. . . . O.K. Ellie, I accept. But there's one condition.

ELLIE. Anything you say, Henry.

HENRY. We got to do this like the big judgin' in the city.

ELLIE. Sure, Henry.

HENRY. It's customary for the judge to kiss the winner.

ELLIE. Kiss the winner . . . Henry, they don't!

HENRY. Yep. And that's my condition. Either I do . . . or I don't.

ELLIE. I don't understand what you mean?

HENRY. Either I do kiss the winner or I don't do the judgin'.

ELLIE. Well, it's all right with me, Henry, if that's the way you want it . . . And if your missus don't object.

HENRY. That's the way I want it . . . according to the rules. Where you holding the show?

ELLIE. Usual place. Down in the big barn. And with your conditions I'll bet the biggest attraction at the fair will be the hog judgin'. (*Quick curtain as* ELLIE *turns to leave and* ZEKE *roars with laughter.*)

SUGGESTIONS

You have no narrator here. The dialogue carries the story, and the puppeteers will have to speak up. There is an opportunity to characterize Henry, Zeke, and Ellie, too, pointing up the difference between the slow-talking Zeke and the loud, self-confident Henry. Ellie, of course, can be a gusher.

You need so little in the way of costume—checked shirts on the men and perhaps a straw hat on one of them. Zeke might have a beard.

Ellie needs a sunbonnet and a shawl around her shoulders. Her bag of doughnuts will add a good touch. You can mold the doughnuts out of clay or, better yet, use Styrofoam.

TILLIE'S TERROR

CHARACTERS

THE NARRATOR, NOT A PUPPET

TILLIE, THE HEROINE

BERTRAM, THE HERO

THE GHOST

CYRUS GULCH, THE BRUSH MAN

RUDOLPH, THE VILLAIN

The NARRATOR *steps in front of the audience while the puppet theater curtain is still closed.*

NARRATOR. Ladies and gentlemen, some of you may have seen the melodramas of long ago: *East Lynn, The Perils of Pauline.* They are being revived constantly across the country. And now with your kind permission we should like to present one of our own entitled, *Tillie's Terror* or *Why Did He Leave Her Alone?*

Our scene is laid in the big house on the hill. Tillie, our heroine, and her husband, Bertram, have rented the rambling old mansion for the winter. It looked all right in the daytime, but by night it is dark and lonely. What's more, it is haunted, but no one told Tillie and Bertram about the ghost.

It is a stormy night, naturally, but since the cupboard is bare, Bertram had to go off to the village for supplies.

"Don't let anyone in," he warned her, "until I return." Poor Tillie is left alone, and there is something else she doesn't know. Rudolph, the villain, who has been pursuing her for years, has followed them here.

It is blowing up a gale. (*wind noise*) Bertram has been gone for hours, and as our curtains part we find poor Tillie watching from the window. (*Curtain opens.* TILLIE *is at the window.*) Why, oh why, doesn't Bertram come home? Tillie tries to sing, but her voice breaks.

TILLIE. (*starts to sing but gives up*)

NARRATOR. She paces the floor to keep up her courage.

TILLIE. (*moves back and forth across the stage*)

NARRATOR. She has an uncanny feeling that she is being observed.

(*The* GHOST *enters and floats behind* TILLIE.)

NARRATOR. Then suddenly there is a knock at the door. Tillie is startled. Who can it be? She forgets Bertram's advice. Timidly she tiptoes to the door and opens it just a crack.

TILLIE. (*shows surprise with a toss of her head and goes to open the door*)

NARRATOR. A long nose pokes into the room.

(*The long nose of* CYRUS GULCH *pokes onto the stage.*)

NARRATOR. Wait a minute, there is a man at the other end of the nose. Yes, we recognize him now. It is Cyrus Gulch, the brush salesman. (CYRUS *enters*) But Tillie doesn't need any brushes. "Go," she says.

TILLIE. (*shakes her head and flings her arm toward the door*)

NARRATOR. "Just let me show you," he insists.

CYRUS. (*shoves one of his brushes in* TILLIE'*s face*)

NARRATOR. "Go," she says again. She pushes Cyrus to the door.

TILLIE. (*pushes* CYRUS *toward the door*)

NARRATOR. He pushes her back.

CYRUS. (*pushes* TILLIE *back to center stage*)

NARRATOR. Back and forth they go. (CYRUS *and* TILLIE *push each other back and forth from one side of the puppet stage to the other.*)

NARRATOR. Finally, with a mighty effort Tillie gets ahold of the nose. She gives it a good tweak.

TILLIE. (*grabs* CYRUS GULCH'*s nose and twists it*)

NARRATOR. Cyrus lets out a yell and runs from the house.

CYRUS. (*yells and exits*)

NARRATOR. Weak with the struggle, poor Tillie drops to the floor exhausted. And the storm rages.

TILLIE. (*falls, hanging over the edge of the puppet stage*)

(*There is the sound of thunder.*)

NARRATOR. There is another knock. (*knock*) Tillie leaps to her feet.

TILLIE. (*rises up again, cupping her hand to her ear*)

NARRATOR. Should she? Or should she not? Again she tiptoes to the door.

TILLIE. (*goes to the door*)

NARRATOR. No one there. But Tillie feels certain that she is not alone.

GHOST. (*enters and floats across the stage over* TILLIE'S *head*)

NARRATOR. Tillie tries to sing again.

TILLIE. (*starts to sing, but her voice cracks again*)

NARRATOR. Another knock. (*There is a knock at the door.*) She is braver now. It is probably only the wind. She opens the door, and in stalks a sinister figure.

TILLIE. (*goes to the door and* RUDOLPH *stalks in*)

NARRATOR. It is Rudolph, the villain. He has been lurking about the house and now he has come to carry Tillie away with him.

RUDOLPH. (*moves toward* TILLIE)

NARRATOR. She shrinks back in fright. If only Bertram would return.

TILLIE. (*shrinks away from* RUDOLPH *and shakes her head*)

NARRATOR. Rudolph laughs.

RUDOLPH. (*laughs*)

NARRATOR. Tillie screams.

TILLIE. (*screams*)

NARRATOR. Rudolph laughs again.

RUDOLPH. (*laughs again*)

NARRATOR. Tillie screams again.

TILLIE. (*screams again*)

NARRATOR. Rudolph is strong and he is wicked. If only Bertram would return. Rudolph sweeps Tillie into his arms and is about to flee with her.

RUDOLPH. (*picks up* TILLIE *and starts toward the door*)

NARRATOR. But the door opens. Sure enough there is our hero with his arms full of groceries.

BERTRAM. (*enters with the bag of groceries*)

NARRATOR. Bertram drops his bundle of groceries.

BERTRAM. (*drops the bag*)

NARRATOR. Rudolph drops Tillie.

RUDOLPH. (*drops* TILLIE)

NARRATOR. They struggle, and Bertram drags Rudolph out into the storm.

BERTRAM and RUDOLPH. (*struggle and* BERTRAM *pulls* RUDOLPH *out the door as the thunder is heard*)

NARRATOR. Dear, dear, Bertram. (BERTRAM *reenters.*) And now our hero and heroine rush into each other's arms.

BERTRAM and TILLIE. (*rush into each other's arms*)

NARRATOR. And neither of them see the white figure which floats above their heads.

GHOST. (*floats across the stage above the heads of* TILLIE *and* BERTRAM)

NARRATOR. But ladies and gentlemen, they need not be afraid. It is only the ghost of Old Aunt Emily. She was watching over them all the time. The end.

(*Curtain closes.*)

SUGGESTIONS

The narrator should be dressed in the fashion of the early 1900's—a checked vest maybe and a high stiff collar. He might have a watch and chain. Remember this is melodrama. Speeches, gestures, emotion are all exaggerated.

It isn't necessary to have any kind of backdrop scene for the puppet theater unless you want the window. Concentrate on costuming the puppets. Tillie, with leg-o-mutton sleeves on a high-necked blouse, would surely have golden hair piled up on top her head. Bertram's brown hair should be parted in the middle, and he could have a vest over a white shirt. The ghost is simple, just white sheeting with black painted rounds for eyes and mouth. Cyrus Gulch must have a long, long nose and carry a little sample case as well as the brush he pokes in Tillie's face. Rudolph could have a black mustache and maybe a top hat and cape.

Bertram's bag of groceries is important and could be filled with bits of carrot tops and spinach. These will, of course, spill out when the bag is dropped—good for a laugh.

As the skit is presented here the narrator has all the lines, and the puppeteers do the singing, screaming, laughing. You can, however, have the puppets speak. Just be sure they can be heard. And don't forget the sound effects: the wind, the rain, and the thunder.

SHOES AND SHIPS AND A MERMAID

CHARACTERS

CAPTAIN KIDD (JUST THE HEAD OF THE PIRATE)

LONG JOHN SILVER (ALSO JUST THE HEAD)

SAILOR BILL

FIRST SAILOR

SECOND SAILOR

SEAWEED SAM, AN OLD SALT WITH A POCKETFUL OF TALES

DAVY JONES, GUARDIAN OF THE DEEP

MILDRED, THE MERMAID, BEAUTIFUL, JUST BEAUTIFUL

OZZIE, THE OCTOPUS

As the play opens the curtain of the puppet stage is closed. The head of CAPTAIN KIDD *appears through the opening.*

CAPTAIN KIDD. Sh! Sh! Quiet everybody. You'll have to excuse my coming out just this far. I'm only a head, you see. It's embarrassing too. I am supposed to introduce the show, and I can't even put in a proper appearance.

LONG JOHN. (*poking his head out also, somewhat above* KIDD) Well, if you're going to complain about it, let somebody else in. I'm just dead weight back here, you know.

CAPTAIN KIDD. Oh, that word. Don't ever say that word again.

LONG JOHN. Dead! Dead! Dead! You might as well face it. We're both dead as door nails, you know. Go on. Get on with the show. Everybody's waiting.

CAPTAIN KIDD. The show tonight is about the sea. There's this sailor, Bill, see, who wants to . . .

LONG JOHN. Don't give away the plot. Just tell them the name of the thing. Somebody certainly made a mistake when they gave this job to you.

CAPTAIN KIDD. All right! All right! The play for tonight is entitled, *Shoes and Ships and a Mermaid.*

LONG JOHN. Or *Come on Down, the Water's Fine.* Watch for us now, folks. We may be dead, but we're in it. (*Both heads withdraw.*)

(*The curtain opens on* SCENE ONE. *This is the deck of a ship and can best be indicated by a backdrop of sea and sky and a ship's rail. The* TWO SAILORS *enter singing—any nursery rhyme tune which fits the words will do.*)

SAILORS.

Two of the jolliest sailors are we
Sailing on top of the rolling blue sea.
Some sailor boys want to see Davy Jones
But we could . . .

FIRST SAILOR. Shh . . . look! Here comes Sailor Bill. All he talks about is the bottom of the sea . . . says he wants to see the mermaid.

SECOND SAILOR. He's crazy. Let's hide. (*They exit right.*)

(BILL *enters and after looking wistfully out over the water turns to the audience.*)

BILL. Gee, it's no fun up here. I sure wish I could see the bottom of the sea. Seaweed Sam says it's wonderful, and he ought to know. He's been there. Golly, here he comes now.

SAM. (*enters*) Hello there, Billy. Why so sad?

BILL. I been thinkin' about that mermaid, Mildred. Sam, does she really and truly have a tail?

SAM. Sure she has a tail . . . a long shimmering tail.

BILL. Tell me the rest, Sam.

SAM. Well . . . her face is like an angel. And she has long golden hair. And her voice . . . boy, when she talks . . . say, look here young fellow, I told you all this just yesterday.

BILL. I just like to hear it again, that's all.

SAM. (*carried away with his story*) By gum (*he looks out over the rail*) if this ain't just about the spot where she lives.

BILL. Sam, I've decided. A sailor can't stay on top of the sea all the time. I'm going down. You wait here while I get my diving helmet.

SAM. Look here, now. You ain't really goin' down there. It's a long way to the bottom . . . and a longer way back.

BILL. If Mildred is as beautiful as you say, maybe I won't come back. (*He exits left, calling back over his shoulder.*) I'll only be a few minutes.

SAM. Now what have I done? I'd better stop him. Hey there, Billy, wait for me. (*Exits.*)

(*The* TWO SAILORS *enter.*)

FIRST SAILOR. Did you hear what I heard?

SECOND SAILOR. Now I know he's crazy. (*They sing.*)
Some sailor boys want to see Davy Jones,
But we could tell them he's nothing but bones.
As for the mermaid he's anxious to meet,
We'll take a girl who has legs and two feet.

(*They exit.* BILL *enters from the left. He wears a diving helmet, and* SAM *follows behind him, out of breath.*)

SAM. Now look, I wouldn't go down there if I was you.

BILL. You did.

SAM. You shouldn't believe everything you hear . . . especially from me.

BILL. Don't try to stop me, Sam. You're just sorry you're too old to go again. (*Exits right.*)

SAM. (*shouts after him*) Doggone it. It's cold down there, and you'll get your feet wet. (*speaks to audience*) I've never been to the bottom of the sea . . . but it made a good story . . . (*he shouts after* BILL) Well, if you find Mildred, give her my love. (*Exits left. Curtain.*)

(SCENE TWO *is at the bottom of the sea and* BILL *enters as the curtain opens. All along the back there are pirates' heads on wooden spikes.*)

BILL. Gee, it is wet down here. I've been walking around for hours. No trace of Mildred. And look at all those heads. That one looks like Captain Kidd, and there's Long John Silver. (*Then he sees the placard which hangs at Davy Jones' doorstep. Reads.*) DAVY JONES' LOCKER . . . RING THE BELL. I guess I better.

DAVY. (*entering in answer to the ring*) What is it? Oh, another sailor. Won't you come in and have a cup of tea? That is, if you don't drink *too* much. We're running rather low.

BILL. I'd prefer it if you came out. The outside's bad enough. (*indicates the heads*)

DAVY. Don't you like it? It's called Dead Head Avenue. Pretty good, I think. I named it myself.

BILL. If there's anything I like less than anything, it's heads without bodies.

DAVY. They didn't mind. They were dead before they got to me.

BILL. But why did you cut off their heads?

DAVY. I cut off their heads because I didn't like their feet. You are beginning to bore me. I'm not so sure your head wouldn't look good up there too.

BILL. That would be very unfriendly. Besides I'm not dead.

DAVY. If you displease me, you might as well be. If I don't like someone I send Ozzie the Octopus after him. That does it. Ozzie is invincible . . . *if* he can stay clear of rocks. He trips a lot. By the way, where do you think you're going?

BILL. I'm on my way to see Mildred . . . the mermaid. How do I get there?

DAVY. (*pointing*) Down that way . . . a good three minutes as the fish swim. But Millie is my girl. I'm beginning to dislike you very much. I'm afraid the Octopus will be right behind you.

BILL. Pish, posh, who's afraid of an Octopus? (*Exits.*)

DAVY. (*calling offstage.*) *Ozzie! Ozzie!* (*The* OCTOPUS *enters.*)

OZZIE. (*singing dolefully*)
I'm an Octopus as you can see.
And all of these legs belong to me.
One two three, four five six, seven and eight.
There's surely no reason to ever be late.
Did you call?

DAVY. You are to follow the sailor who just left here. Don't let him get away. And watch your clumsy feet. If you stumble this time you're through.

OZZIE. Can I help it if there's a shoe shortage down here. If I had shoes, it wouldn't hurt so when I stumble on the rocks.

DAVY. Well, keep your feet out of the way. (*Exits.*)

OZZIE. (*mimics*) Keep your feet out of the way. Keep your feet out of the way. That's easy enough to say. But if you had eight instead of two, I wonder if you'd think it easy to do. (*Exits singing "I'm an octopus, etc.," as* BILL *enters from the other side.*)

BILL. I think I'm going around in circles. (*He inspects the locker sign again and then turns to see* OZZIE *who circled around and followed him.*) Oh, oh, Davy Jones is a man of his word. There's the Octopus. But I don't believe he's looking where he's going. I'll just put this stone in his way and wait. (*He puts a rock in the path of the octopus [no need for a real rock—just pretend]*)

OZZIE. (*singing*) I'm an Octopus, and you can see. (*stumbles*) Oh woe is me, I'm wounded. I'm wounded. I shall probably die . . .

BILL. (*mimics*) He's an Octopus and you can see
He cannot get the best of me. (*Exits.*)

OZZIE. Wait! Wait for me. You can't expect me to catch you this way. (*He exits as the curtain closes.*)

(SCENE THREE *is still at the bottom of the sea. The heads are no longer in view. The* MERMAID *sits at one side of the stage.*)

MILDRED. (*singing*)
I'm a maiden fair beneath the sea,
And all of the fishes are good to me.
The Octopus has asked my hand;
I'd rather marry a German band.
Eight strong legs are surely more
Than any mermaid would bargain for.
Besides I'm promised to Davy Jones,
A pretty good guy in spite of his bones.

BILL. (*enters from the left*) Oh dear, do turn around so that I can be sure.

MILDRED. Turn around? (*She turns.*)

BILL. Don't talk yet. I'm taking one thing at a time. It's true. You do have a tail, and it shimmers. Now you can talk.

MILDRED. I think you're quite impertinent.

BILL. Much, much better than I expected. Let me see, the hair is next . . . long, golden, beautiful.

MILDRED. Thank you. Of course, if I hadn't lost my comb, I could keep it in better condition. Combs are hard to get down here.

BILL. Everything checks all right. May I stay awhile?

MILDRED. You aren't selling anything?

BILL. Of course not. I'm a sailor.

MILDRED. That's unfortunate. Ozzie usually goes after the sailors. He's Davy's right-hand man, and Davy doesn't care much for sailors. Ozzie's the Octopus, you know . . . wants to marry me.

BILL. You won't?

MILDRED. No. Too many legs. No. I'll probably marry Davy in a hundred years or so. A girl can't wait too long.

BILL. Aren't you going to invite me in to tea?

MILDRED. Tea! I haven't any tea. Not any more. Somebody threw a whole boatload down to us some time ago, and we drank tea like crazy for awhile. But now Davy has all that's left. You may have a dish of seaweed though, if you like.

BILL. (*grimaces by covering his face with his hands*) Very like spinach, I suppose. No thank you. Oh, oh, here comes Ozzie. Don't let him take me. I'll hide out here. (*Exits right.*)

OZZIE. (*Moaning as he enters from the left. He is holding one foot.*) Oh, dear! Oh, dear! The sailor wounded me. Two swords and a gun he had. Did he come in here? I lost him.

MILDRED. Why, the little bully. (*to audience*) He didn't say anything to me about that. (*to* OZZIE) You go on in my house over there (*points off left*) and bandage your leg. I'll get the sailor for you. He should be taught a lesson.

OZZIE. Promise you'll get him. Davy says I'm *through* if I don't bring in that sailor.

MILDRED. I'll call you when he's ready for delivery. (OZZIE *exits limping.*) Sailor! Sailor! You can come out now.

BILL. (*enters again and looks off to the left*) Has he gone?

MILDRED. Don't worry about him. Come here. I want to get a better look at you.

BILL. Gee.

MILDRED. Take off your head . . . (*she reaches for the helmet*)

BILL. No, you don't. I like my head *and* my feet. I want them close together.

MILDRED. I mean this bubble head, silly.

BILL. Oh gee, no, I can't take that off.

MILDRED. I can't very well love a sailor with a bowl on his head.

BILL. Oh, well . . . if that's the way you feel . . . gee! (MILDRED *pulls off the helmet and* BILL *gurgles and keels over.*)

MILDRED. Dummy! (*calls to* OZZIE) O.K., Ozzie, come and get him.

(OZZIE *comes in from left with bandaged leg. He drags* BILL *off and the curtain falls as* MILDRED *sings "I'm a maiden fair, etc."*)

(SCENE FOUR *is outside* DAVY'S *locker again.* OZZIE *is alone.*)

OZZIE. (*shouting through the entrance to the locker*) Off with his head! Off with his head!

DAVY. (*poking his head into view*) That's from *Alice in Wonderland*. You read too much.

OZZIE. Well, it's a good idea. What are you going to do with him?

DAVY. Don't be in a hurry. This is a most important case. The best we've had in a thousand years.

OZZIE. I'm the one who was wounded. Don't I have anything to say?

DAVY. Don't worry. We have your interests at heart. (*pulls his head in*)

OZZIE. Well, anyhow, I have the bubble hat. I could use it as an umbrella, except that it never rains at the bottom of the sea. It's too big for a shoe, and besides I'd need eight of them. I tell you it's rough to be an Octopus.

DAVY. (*enters from doorway of locker*) We've decided to send the sailor back. May I have his hat, please?

OZZIE. I don't think that's fair. He should be made to suffer. Look at my poor leg.

DAVY. You've got more legs than you need anyhow. Besides he has promised to drop us a few pounds of tea and a comb for Millie's hair.

OZZIE. How about me? Don't I get anything?

DAVY. Well, he did say something about shoes.

OZZIE. Four pair!

DAVY. They won't all match, but he said he'd do the best he could. (DAVY *takes the diving helmet and exits.*)

OZZIE. I'm going to get shoes. I'm going to get shoes. I'm so happy I could cry. (*And he does just that as the curtain closes.*) (SCENE FIVE *is back on the deck of the ship again.*)

SAM. (*looks out over the rail and then paces back and forth*) Oh, dear. I know he'll get his feet wet. It's all my fault. He probably won't ever get back . . . and if he does he'll probably have pneumonia. (BILL *enters and* SAM *rushes to him, patting him on the back.*) Thank goodness. You had me so worried. . . . Why, you're not wet at all.

BILL. Well, it seemed wet at first . . . but after you get used to it . . . and of course it never rains down there . . .

SAM. You have a bad dent in your diving helmet. What happened?

BILL. Ozzie tried to use it as a shoe. It got kicked about a bit. I doubt whether I should have been able to get it back at all if I'd had eight of them. Ozzie needs shoes.

People just aren't throwing shoes over the side any more . . . especially eight at a time. It is such a disadvantage to need so many.

SAM. (*to audience*) Poor Billy. His brain is affected. I'll humor him. What's that in your hand? (*He points to the seaweed* BILL *clutches.*)

BILL. It's spinach . . . I mean seaweed. Really good. I had some before I left. I've grown quite fond of it.

SAM. Don't you think you'd better lie down . . . you don't feel sick?

BILL. Sick! Oh dear, I just remembered. I think, perhaps, I may be dead. Oh well, it hasn't interfered with my appetite. I'm hungry. A lovely dish of seaweed and a cup of tea. That's what I need. Poor Davy. The tea *is* running low. I must see to it.

SAM. (*to audience*) I'll put him to the real test. (*to* BILLY) Did you see Mildred . . . the mermaid?

BILL. Mildred. Her hair so long and golden . . . just as you said. And she hasn't a comb. I must see to that too. Remind me to send her one as a wedding gift. She is marrying Davy Jones, you know. And I am invited to the wedding. (*sneezes*) Goodness, it's damp up here. And now you'll have to excuse me. It is quite possible that I am dead, and I am very, very hungry. (*Exits.*)

SAM. (*to audience*) Sad. But don't worry. I'll have him back in shape in no time. (*Follows* BILL *off*. TWO SAILORS *enter.*)

SAILORS. (*singing*)

Some sailor boys want to see Davy Jones,
But we could tell them he's nothing but bones.
We'd so much rather stay right where we be,
Sailing on top of the rolling blue sea.

(SAM *enters from the right in great haste.*)

SAM. (*to the audience*) Hang onto your shoes! Hang onto your shoes! He's comin' this way. (*The* SAILORS *exit left as* BILL *enters with his arms full of shoes.*)

BILL. (*to audience*) Just a few more . . . that's all Ozzie needs. . . . As soon as I throw these over the side I'll come out there and take what you can give me. (*He exits as the curtain falls.*)

SUGGESTIONS

This is longer than the other puppet shows. There are more lines, and the puppet characters have greater opportunities to act. The props are not difficult; the most important are the shoes for the final scene. You can probably find doll shoes that will work nicely.

You will have to spend more time making the puppets. The two sailors and Bill are easy enough. Just vary hair color and the shape of the heads. Seaweed Sam is an old salt with beard and a pipe, and Captain Kidd and Long

John Silver (who are just heads) can have eye patches and earrings and kerchief headpieces. The mermaid's tail can be part of the front body section and can be flipped over the edge of the stage for all to appreciate. The octopus can have a round head and tentacles of stuffed muslin strips which are given flexibility with wire. The puppeteer's hand would fit up into the head. Finally, why not paint a skeleton in luminous white paint on black material for Davy? That should provide his "nothing but bones" image.

PART IV

THE VARIETY PROGRAM

THE VARIETY PROGRAM

. . . everyone for himself . . .

The variety program needs no definition. It is exactly what the name suggests, and most people are familiar with the talent show, for example, which is given a unity by the master of ceremonies who introduces each performer in turn.

If you have experimented with pantomime and the simple puppet play, you are ready for the kind of entertainment in which each person has a separate act or piece of the show. He will probably have lines to learn and action to carry out, but he is responsible for his own performance only. He can build it up or play it down as he chooses. If he does well, everyone will be pleased. If he muffs things, the whole program isn't ruined.

When there are lines to speak, the important thing is volume. You want to be heard. But the variety show also allows for parts which have no voice if someone prefers it that way.

You still have the narrator, the master of ceremonies, the storyteller, whatever he happens to be in your particular production. He will hold things together. Sometimes there is a thread of connection between the acts. Sometimes they are unrelated.

And anyone can be the star.

MRS. CLOPSADDLE PRESENTS SPRING

Characters

ANNOUNCER

MRS. CLOPSADDLE, A GUSHY ELOCUTION TEACHER OF THE EARLY 1900's

SUSAN, WHO HAS A COLD

PATRICIA, THE SHY ONE, MAKING HER FIRST APPEARANCE

GENEVIEVE, THE DANCER

THE CAST OF THE PLAY, *Spring Garden*

- THE VIOLET
- THE SWEETPEA
- THE DAFFODIL
- THE TULIP
- THE DAISY
- THE WORM
- THE GARDENER

ANNOUNCER. There may be none of you who remember, but back in the early years of the twentieth century in cities and towns all over America there existed something called "the school of elocution." It was there that children were taught to speak pieces and recite poems and to give plays. For your entertainment we'd like to take you back to those days as Mrs. Clopsaddle and her pupils present Spring.

(MRS. CLOPSADDLE *enters from the left in front of the closed curtain. The* ANNOUNCER *nods to her and exits.*)

MRS. CLOPSADDLE. Good evening, ladies and gentlemen. What a pleasure it is to welcome all the dear parents of my lovely, lovely, children. (*She looks out over the audience and spots someone.*) Oh, I see you are here, Mrs. Snodgrass. I want to speak to you after the program. But we must get on now, because we have a good deal of talent here. Let me see. (*She adjusts her glasses and inspects her paper.*) Our first entertainer this evening is Susan Green. She has a poem for us.

SUSAN. (*Enters sniffling. She has a cold, and there is a man-sized handkerchief pinned to her dress.*)

Spring! Spring!
Beautiful spring!
Season of happiness,
What do you bring? (*She draws her finger across her nose.*)

MRS. CLOPSADDLE. (*interrupting*) Use your handkerchief, dear . . . your handkerchief.

SUSAN. (*paying no attention*)

Blossoms of violet,
Tulip and rose,
Songs of the birds,
And a cold in the nose. (*She sneezes and runs off.*)

MRS. CLOPSADDLE. (*applauds with the audience*) She really has a cold, you know. Just right for the part. (*She laughs.*) And now, little Patricia Spencer in her very first appearance. (*She beckons to someone off-stage and finally goes over to bring* PATRICIA *out.*)

PATRICIA. (*Very shyly she begins to speak, twisting the skirt of her dress.*) I'm a . . . (*she falters*) . . . I'm a little . . . (*she stops again*) . . . I'm a little honey . . . (*She bites her nails, starts to cry and finally runs off sobbing.*)

MRS. CLOPSADDLE. Well, as I said, this is Patricia's first appearance . . . (*aside*) It may be her last . . . (*then aloud again*) I guess we're all shy sometimes, aren't we? Now we're ready to trip the light fantastic. (*She does a dance step to demonstrate her enthusiasm for her pupils.*) Genevieve Lewis will honor us with "The Dance of the Butterflies."

(*This is an opportunity for bringing in a little action without words. There is always someone who can't or won't learn a line but loves to perform. The dance can be as laughable as you wish to make it.* GENEVIEVE *stumbles over her own feet and is out of step with the music, which can be live or recorded. She also has trouble with her headdress falling down over her eyes.*)

MRS. CLOPSADDLE. (*watching her*) Isn't she sweet? (*When* GENEVIEVE *finishes there is applause and* MRS. CLOPSADDLE *consults her program.*) Oh yes, the highlight of our evening . . . a little drama of the flowers. I'll introduce the performers later, but at this time we present *Spring Garden.*

(MRS. CLOPSADDLE *steps aside as* THE VIOLET *comes on.*)

THE VIOLET. I'm a violet, and I'm shy. I don't care if nobody picks me . . . or even sees me down here in the tall grass. Of course, I wouldn't mind being in a May basket, maybe with a little clover. But I'm so small, and I'm just lost in a crowd. I'm shy.

(THE VIOLET *stoops down and hides her face as* THE SWEETPEA *enters.*)

THE SWEETPEA. (*bounces in and poses as though climbing up a fence or trellis*) Well, I want to be seen and picked too. I climb up the fences and burst out in a glory of color. And I'll bet the sweetpea is about the first spring flower you can put in a bouquet. I smell nice, too.

(THE SWEETPEA *stays on the stage along with* THE VIOLET *as* THE DAFFODIL *enters.*)

THE DAFFODIL. (*with a Southern accent*) I'm a daffodil, and they can say all they want about color, but be honest now, is there anything brighter than yellow?

(THE TULIP *enters with a stately bearing.*)

THE TULIP. It isn't until you've seen a tulip that you've seen a *real* flower. All dignity and grace. You certainly wouldn't catch me hiding in the grass. And as for climbing fences . . . how unladylike. (*She takes her place on the stage with the others.*)

(THE DAISY *tiptoes in and rolls her eyes knowingly before she speaks.*)

THE DAISY. I'm a daisy . . . (*pause*) . . . and I know who's the best in the garden . . . (*then with a sly smile*) But I won't tell.

(THE WORM *enters with a slithering movement. He has a napkin tied around his neck and brandishes a knife and fork.*)

THE WORM. Boy, am I hungry. (*He smacks his lips and moves toward the flowers. They cringe in fear.*)

(THE GARDENER *in straw hat and overalls enters. He has a small spade and a can. He talks to himself.*)

THE GARDENER. There'll be no pests in my garden. Any big fat worms will make fishing bait. I'll see to that.

(THE WORM *heads for the exit as quickly as he can as* THE FLOWERS *cheer and the curtain falls.* MRS. CLOPSADDLE *calls the play cast back for introductions. The players' real names might by used.*)

MRS. CLOPSADDLE. I guess that concludes our program for the evening . . . (*There is a frantic whispering from off-stage.* MRS. CLOPSADDLE *goes to investigate and then returns.*) Well, little Patricia is going to try again. Come on, dear. We're waiting. (*Someone pushes* PATRICIA *onto the stage.*)

PATRICIA. (*still as shy as before and as miserable*) I'm a

little honey bee . . . (*She gets that much out fast and then falters.*) who's . . . who's . . .

(*A voice from the wings prompts in a loud voice.*)

VOICE. Who's wandered from the comb.

ALL THE FLOWERS. (*peeking out at the sides of the stage*)
And this would be a better show
If she had stayed at home.

(PATRICIA *runs off the stage crying at the top of her lungs.*)

MRS. CLOPSADDLE. Now that really is the end of our show. (*She makes a deep curtsy; then remembering Mrs. Snodgrass, she speaks out to the crowd again.*) Don't leave, Mrs. Snodgrass. Remember, I must speak to you. (*She exits.*)

SUGGESTIONS

Since this is definitely set in an earlier time, half of the humor will lie in the costuming and the exaggerated characterizations. Pick a time that interests you and look up a bit about the dress of that period, maybe 1912. Give Mrs. Clopsaddle a hobble-skirted gown with a high neckline and let her use a lorgnette. The girls would have long stockings, sailor-collared dresses perhaps, and the boys knee pants.

The flowers in the little play identify themselves with their lines. You could have them carry the kind of flower they portray or provide costumes that would be appropriate. The violet, for example, in a violet color, the sweetpea with a pink sunbonnet, the daffodil in a bright yellow dress, the tulip with a collar that stands up around her face like the petals of the bloom she represents. The daisy could have a halo crown of daisies, and the worm . . . well, there's the fun. How about a long gray T-shirt. He walks with a slithering movement, of course, and has that napkin tied around his neck. Don't forget the knife and fork.

STORIES TO REMEMBER

CHARACTERS

ANNOUNCER

The first story: The Umbrella

PAMELA POTTER

HER FRIEND

The second story: The Cookie Jar

JEFFERSON JACKSON

HIS FRIEND

The third story: The Easter Egg Hunt

PENELOPE PERKINS

The fourth story: The Harmonica

HERMAN HOGELMEYER

THE OTHER BOY

The fifth story: The Beautiful Clothes

THE CLEVER GIRL

LADY ELEGANT

In each of the stories, the speaker is narrator and player. He performs the actions and expresses the feelings as he describes them and delivers the speeches as though he is appearing in a play.

(*The* ANNOUNCER *enters in front of the closed curtain.*)

ANNOUNCER. The little stories we have to tell you tonight are with all due respect, or perhaps I should say apology, to Aesop. Our first story: *The Umbrella.*

(*As the curtain opens on the first story,* PAMELA *enters.*)

PAMELA POTTER. When Pamela Potter was ten years old, in fact on the very day of her birthday, her best friend came over to see her. She brought a present. (*As she says these words* PAMELA *goes to exit right and ushers her friend in.*) Pamela was very excited about the present because it was an odd-shaped package. She said, "I wonder what it can be." And then Pamela and her friend opened the box together. There lay a beautiful umbrella. "What a beautiful umbrella," said Pamela, taking it out and opening it up. Then she strolled around the room with it over her head.

While Pamela was admiring the umbrella, it started to rain, and Pamela's friend had to go home. Of course she asked to borrow the umbrella so that she wouldn't get wet. But Pamela refused. "It's mine. You just gave it to me. Why should I let you take it?" And so her friend pulled her sweater up over her head and ran home in the rain (*the* FRIEND *does this and exits*) while Pamela stayed in her warm dry house with her umbrella. (*Curtain closes as* PAMELA *folds the umbrella and puts it back in the box.*)

ANNOUNCER. Our second story: *The Cookie Jar.*

(*The curtain opens as* JEFFERSON JACKSON *enters with his friend.*)

JEFFERSON JACKSON. One day Jefferson Jackson said to his friend, "Come on. My mother baked cookies today.

We'll get some." He told his friend to follow him to the kitchen. There was the cookie jar high up on the shelf. Jefferson Jackson stood on tiptoe, but he wasn't tall enough. He said, "I'll have to get a chair." And Jefferson Jackson found a chair, climbed up on it, and tried again, but still the cookie jar was out of reach. He said to his friend, "I'll put a book on the chair." And he did just that. He found a big book, but it was still no good. The cookie jar was beyond his fingers. Well, Jefferson Jackson hopped down and shrugged his shoulders. "Come on," he said to his friend. "I don't think my mother made the kind of cookies we like anyhow." (*Exit as curtain closes.*)

ANNOUNCER. Our third story: *The Easter Egg Hunt.*

(*Curtain opens and* PENELOPE PERKINS *enters.*)

PENELOPE PERKINS. It was Easter week, and there was a great party in the auditorium at school. Everybody was invited to come and hunt for the candy eggs hidden around the room. There were only two rules. You could have only what you could carry, and when the whistle blew you had to stop and keep only what you had. Now Penelope came to the party with a big apron on so that she could gather more candy eggs than anyone else. When the signal was given to start, she ran about the room, picking up first one and another until her apron was full and so heavy she could hardly hold it up. Then she spied one extra-large candy egg at the back of the room. She hurried over to get it, pushing her way through the crowds of children . . . rather rudely. She bent to pick up that last egg when the weight of the others she had caused her to lose her grip on her apron (of course she was holding it with only one hand) and all of her candy eggs rolled to the floor just as the whistle blew. And there stood Penelope without a single egg in her apron or in her hand. (*Curtain closes.*)

ANNOUNCER. Our fourth story: *The Harmonica.*

(*Curtain opens and* HERMAN HOGELMEYER *enters.*)

HERMAN HOGELMEYER. Herman Hogelmeyer was walking through the park one day when he spotted a harmonica in his path. "Someone must have thrown it away," he said. "I've always wanted to play the harmonica." And he picked it up and played a simple little tune. "I'll practice and practice, and when I play on the street, people will throw coins to me." And Herman Hogelmeyer put down the harmonica and began gathering up the imaginary coins around him. Then he said to himself, "I will use this money to buy a flute. I like a flute even better than I do a harmonica. With a flute I can play in an orchestra." And Herman practiced on his imaginary flute as he skipped down the path. "Finally," he said to himself, "I'll be asked to play a solo, and I'll be rich and famous." Well, Herman Hogelmeyer imagined himself on the great stages of the world, bowing and bowing, and then he remembered that all this would come about because of the harmonica, and he hurried back along the path to get it. But another boy came along just then and picked up the harmonica and carried it away with him. (*The* OTHER BOY *enters, takes the harmonica and exits.*) And when Herman arrived at the spot where he had left his prize it was gone, and he went home shaking his head sadly because he was empty-handed. (*Exits as curtain closes.*)

ANNOUNCER. Our fifth and last story: *The Beautiful Clothes.*

(*The curtain opens as the* CLEVER GIRL *enters from the left. She wears a thin dress, no coat, and she shivers because it is cold.*)

CLEVER GIRL. Long ago there was a Clever Girl. She was very poor, but she dreamed of having fine clothes to wear. She knew, of course, there wasn't much chance, but one day she met Lady Elegant on the outskirts of the village. (LADY ELEGANT *enters.*) She was dressed in elegant clothes, a beautiful coat, a great brimmed hat with sweeping feathers and long white gloves. Just then an idea came to the Clever Girl. She curtsied ever so daintily, and said, "Lady Elegant, how beautiful you look." Then she walked back and forth to admire Lady Elegant from several angles. "You have such a magnificent hat," she said, "but it is such a shame that it hides your shining hair. Yes, it's too bad, but . . . " And Lady Elegant removed her hat, set it down on the ground, and began fluffing up her hair. (LADY ELEGANT *removes her hat.*) Then the Clever Girl said, "That is ever so much better." And this time she walked all around Lady Elegant to admire her. "Yes, it's much better, but still your hands are covered with gloves, and no one can see your long tapering fingers. But I guess it's the way you want it." And without a word, Lady Elegant slipped the gloves off her hands and put them with the hat. (LADY ELEGANT *removes her gloves.*) "Ah," said the Clever Girl, and quite boldly she ventured to touch the hands of Lady Elegant. Then she walked around her again. "Now," she said finally, "if people could only see what a figure you conceal beneath that bulky coat." And the Clever Girl stood back and waited. Of course she did not wait long. Lady Elegant swept the coat from her shoulders and tossed it with the other things. (LADY ELEGANT *does this.*) "There," said the Clever Girl. "What a beauty you are. You must hurry off to the village to show the townspeople. And off Lady Elegant went, shivering a little, because it was cold. (LADY ELEGANT *exits.*) And the Clever Girl smiled and put on all the fine things that were on the ground and went her way, warm and comfortable and elegant with the feathered hat sitting atop her clever, clever head. (*Exits as the curtain closes.*)

Suggestions

Remember that the speaker in each story narrates *and* acts. It will be better if the line is spoken first, followed by the appropriate action. For example: "Jefferson Jackson found a chair, climbed up on it, and tried again." The speaker pauses, gets the chair, and climbs up on it before he resumes the tale. Add more movement and gestures if you wish. The stories are wide open for further development. In fact, you may want to come up with fables of your own.

The costumes and props you need are indicated in the script. An umbrella in its box, the candy eggs (they could be imaginary, but much more fun if they really tumble out of the apron at the end), the harmonica. Penelope must wear an apron and Lady Elegant's clothes are all important. How about a long velvet coat, evening gloves, and an early 1900's hat with ostrich plumes. She could have shoes with silver buckles too, if you wanted to write an extra line or two.

REPEAT AFTER ME

CHARACTERS

JANE NORTH
MARY SOUTH
HELEN EAST
BETTY WEST
} THE BRIDGE FOURSOME

A, B, C, D, E WHO ARE ALL GOING TO THE STORE

Before the curtain opens, "A" enters from the right and as she goes across the stage to exit left she speaks.

"A." I'm going to the supermarket. I need one pound of sausage, two bottles of ketchup, three cans of soup, and four ears of corn. (*Exits.*)

(*The curtain opens. There are four packing box cubicles in a row on the stage. The front side of each has been removed and replaced with a window shade or at least a curtain which can be pulled down. Above each box is a name.* JANE NORTH *on the far right,* MARY SOUTH *next,* HELEN EAST *next, and finally* BETTY WEST *on the far left. The curtains on the boxes are drawn and as the audience watches, Jane North's curtain is raised to reveal* JANE *at the telephone. She wears a housecoat or robe and a curler bonnet on her head. She dials. There is a ring, and the curtain goes up at the box of* MARY SOUTH, *who picks up the receiver. It is* JANE NORTH *who speaks.*)

JANE NORTH. (*in a tone of exasperation*) Mary? I don't think I can make the bridge game today. Tried to call Betty since it's at her house, but her line was busy. John's folks are coming for the weekend. And wouldn't you know, I think I've broken the leg on that antique chair my mother-in-law gave me. I shouldn't have stood on it. I'm afraid it's gone for sure this time. The repair man is supposed to come for it. If he doesn't I don't know what I'll do. On top of that, my sink backed up. I'm trying to get the plumber. If he can't get here today, I'll have to wait till Monday. By that time there'll be water all over the kitchen floor. If things do work out I'll just come along without calling you again, but you'd better not count on me. Get a substitute. Got to dash. You call Betty. (*She hangs up and the curtains are drawn on* JANE NORTH *and* MARY SOUTH, *but the stage curtain remains open.*)

("B" *enters from the right and moves across the stage.*)

"B." I'm going to the supermarket. I need one pound of sausage, two bottles of ketchup, three cans of soup, four ears of corn, five brown onions, half a dozen eggs, seven baking potatoes, and eight solid tomatoes. (*She counts on her fingers as she names the items. She exits.*)

(*Curtain goes up on* MARY SOUTH. *She dials. There is a ring and the curtain is raised on* HELEN EAST *who picks up her phone.*)

MARY SOUTH. Helen? Message from Jane. She isn't going to make it today. Said to get a substitute. She just called, and she sounded terribly frustrated and in an awful hurry. She thinks she broke her leg. She was standing on that antique chair of hers, and it must have crumbled. That thing's caused more trouble. I wish someone would steal it. Oh, yes, she's having plumbing problems too. The kitchen's flooded. She doesn't know what she'll do if the repair man can't get there today, and I know just how she feels. You can't depend on anyone these days. John's whole family's coming for the weekend too. You'd think he'd call and tell them not to come with Jane not even able to stand up. I don't know. When they passed out brains I think they missed John. By the way she tried to call Betty . . . busy line. I couldn't reach her either. You try. (*Hangs up and the curtains are drawn on* MARY SOUTH *and* HELEN EAST.)

("C" *enters from the right and speaks as she crosses the stage.*)

"C." I'm going to the supermarket. I need one pound of sausage, two bottles of ketchup, three cans of soups, four ears of corn, five brown onions, half a dozen eggs, seven baking potatoes, eight solid tomatoes, nine cucumbers, ten oranges, eleven apples, and a dozen doughnuts. (*Exits left.*)

(*Curtain goes up at* HELEN EAST. *She dials. There is a ring, and the curtain goes up on* BETTY WEST *who picks up her phone.*)

HELEN EAST. (*breathless*) Mary just called. Everybody's been trying to get you. Jane's in an awful state. All the drains in her house backed up. The whole first floor is flooded. She got to the phone to call the plumber, but then she slipped in the water and broke her leg. She must have managed to get hold of Mary before she passed out. And wouldn't you know, John's folks are coming down this weekend. They've planned a big family reunion. And as if that isn't enough, someone she thought was a repair man came in and stole that antique chair John's mother gave her. Well, you can see she's not going to make bridge. She's all tied up. We ought to go over there and see if we can help. (HELEN *hangs up and the curtains are drawn on* HELEN EAST *and* BETTY WEST.)

(*"D" enters from the right and goes across the stage as the others before him.*)

"D." I'm going to the supermarket. I need one pound of sausage, two bottles of ketchup, three cans of soup, four ears of corn, five brown onions, half a dozen eggs, seven baking potatoes, eight solid tomatoes, nine cucumbers, ten oranges, eleven apples, a dozen doughnuts, thirteen red roses, fourteen green candles, fifteen pounds of sugar, and sixteen pints of pickled pears. (*Exits left.*)

(*Curtain is raised on* BETTY WEST. *She dials. There is a ring and she speaks.*)

BETTY WEST. John? I just thought I'd better let you know about Jane. You'd better get home as quickly as you can. Terrible things have happened to her. All the plumbing has gone crazy. The whole house is filled with water. Jane managed to get to the phone, barely, but she got busy signals. Then she slipped and fell. Broke both legs. She did get the plumber before she passed out. The plumber apparently couldn't come, though . . . he sent a substitute who tied Jane up and stole that antique chair your mother gave you. Jane must have gained consciousness later though, because she got hold of Mary. Mary called Helen. Helen called me. I'm going over right now. Poor Jane. She's probably lying there helpless. Maybe passed out again. You hurry now. (*Hangs up as her curtain is drawn and the main curtain closes.*)

("E" *enters right and speaks as she crosses the stage.*)

"E." I'm going to the supermarket. I need one pound of sausage, two bottles of ketchup, three cans of soup, four ears of corn, five brown onions, half a dozen eggs, seven baking potatoes, eight solid tomatoes, nine cucumbers, ten oranges, eleven apples, a dozen doughnuts, thirteen red roses, fourteen green candles, fifteen pounds of sugar, sixteen pints of pickled pears . . . (*She has reached the left exit. There is a pause as the audience waits for the addition to the list.* "E" *looks out at the audience.*) Well, I need all these things . . . and more. But I'm not going to get them. I've only got a dollar, and I'll be lucky if I can get a loaf of bread. (*Exits quickly.*)

(*Main curtain opens.* BETTY WEST *enters from the right. She carries a pair of crutches, a roaster, a brown bag of groceries, and she is pushing a wheel chair in front of her. She stops at Jane North's box and raps on the edge of the cubicle with one of the crutches. There is no answer. As she raps again she drops the crutch on her foot. She tries to pick it up, and everything she is carrying falls with a clatter. As Jane North's curtain is raised,* BETTY *plops down in the wheel chair, looking wretched with all the clutter about her.* JANE NORTH *steps out of her box. She is dressed for the street.*)

JANE NORTH. (*seeing* BETTY) Betty, Betty, whatever happened to you? Oh, you poor, poor dear. (*She drops to her side as the main curtain closes quickly.*)

SUGGESTIONS

The cartons with their shades, four toy phones (or stage phones if you can get them), and the props for Betty to use in the last scene are about all you need here. The timing is important. Everything should be well paced and move quickly.

The people going to the market can, of course, be boys or girls. And if you want to rewrite the grocery lists, you might come up with better ones, more alliterative, and even with more items. On the other hand, you may want to eliminate the going to the market routine altogether. You could substitute some other diversion, maybe something more related to the skit . . . a procession of people suggested by the phone conversations. "A" might be a telephone man with a phone to install, "B" a plumber carrying a plunger and tool kit, "C" a repair man dragging along a chair with one leg missing, "D" the members of John's family with a lot of luggage, and "E" a burglar with a mask over his eyes and a loot bag over his shoulders. Since none of these characters would speak—they'd simply walk across the stage—the audience could concentrate on the bridge players' words.

AMATEUR NIGHT AT CUCUMBER CENTER

CHARACTERS

ANNOUNCER, WHO INTRODUCES US TO THE EARLY THIRTIES

PROFESSOR PEABODY, THE MASTER OF CEREMONIES, WHO INTRODUCES THE PERFORMERS

THE MAN WITH THE HOOK, WHO SOMETIMES REMOVES THE PERFORMERS

DOLLIE DOBBS, THE SINGER

JOE GIBBONS, THE JUGGLER

OPAL PENNYFEATHER, THE INTERPRETIVE DANCER

FELICIA QUIMBY, THE WOMAN WITH THE DRAMATIC READING

THE MANAGER OF THE THEATER

THE PEOPLE PLANTED IN THE AUDIENCE, TWO OR THREE

The ANNOUNCER, *in modern dress, steps out in front of the closed curtain.*

ANNOUNCER. All of you know what a talent show is. We still have them once in awhile, because they're great fun. But years ago, before television started giving us so much of our entertainment, the talent show was very important. It was particularly popular in small towns where movie houses were few in number and a stage show was scarce indeed. The performers were usually local people, and there was always a master of ceremonies, sometimes brought out from the city, who introduced the various acts, encouraged applause, and kept things moving along. Tonight we'd like to take you back to one of those towns during the early thirties and bring you Professor Peabody and the talent of Cucumber Center.

(*The curtain opens. The* ANNOUNCER *gestures toward the wings opposite him as the* MASTER OF CEREMONIES *enters. The* ANNOUNCER *then exits.*)

MASTER OF CEREMONIES. (*He is a quick stepping, fast talking showman, fired with enthusiasm.*) Good evening, all you fine people of Cucumber Center. I've met a good number of your citizens since I come to town to conduct this talent show, but mostly I guess they been those folks that wanted to be contestants. So let me introduce myself to the rest of you. Professor Peabody. (*There is applause from the* TWO OR THREE PEOPLE *planted in the audience.*) Thank you, thank you. You bet that's the name, folks, Professor H. R. Peabody from Chicago. (*He pronounces it Chicaga.*) Now we're gonna have a show here tonight. . . . Yes, I know there was a little grumbling out in the lobby because you weren't gonna get a movie this week and we aren't gonna give away any free dishes, but, folks, you're gonna see a real live show. And then you're gonna pick a winner and we're gonna take him right on over to Grundy Springs to compete in the county run-offs. And then . . . and *then* some lucky guy . . . or gal . . . is gonna go up to the state competition . . . (*The* MASTER OF CEREMONIES *is interrupted by someone who rushes on stage and hands him a note. He looks at the paper.*) Well now, I do have an announcement. The manager here wants me to tell you he's sorry about this, but we aren't gonna be able to use the applause meter tonight. It's outa kilter, but we'll see to it that you have ballots, and you're gonna vote in writing. You won't know the winner till tomorrow, but there'll be a little extra suspense that way. O.K. now, let's get on with the show. Remember don't sit on your hands. (*He reads off his paper.*) To open the evening, Miss Dollie Dobbs is gonna sing. . . . Well it seems she doesn't give us the number here. We'll have to wait and see.

DOLLIE DOBBS. (*She is, or thinks she is, a soprano. She enters with a sheet of music in her hand. She tries out a high note or two, clears her throat, tries again. Her voice is squeaky and she gets no farther. The people planted in the audience boo, and the* MAN WITH THE HOOK *pulls her off-stage.*)

MASTER OF CEREMONIES. Well, some of them make it and some of them don't. (*looks at his list again*) Now this is a change of pace. Joe Gibbons . . . you all know Joe . . . (*There is a bit of applause.*) He's got a juggling act. Come on out, Joe . . .

JOE GIBBONS. (*Comes on with a basket of balls. He bounces around the stage tossing a couple of them from one hand to the other. Finally he adds a third, and that's where he gets into trouble. All three balls get away from him. He takes more from the basket, tries again. When they're all gone and the basket is empty, the* PEOPLE *in the audi-*

ence boo. The hook comes out but JOE *doesn't wait for it. He runs off the stage on the opposite side, calling out as he goes.*) I did it this morning. I did . . . I really did.

MASTER OF CEREMONIES. (*picks up one of the stray balls*) We better just keep the ball rolling. (*He laughs at his pun.*) O.K. now, Miss Opal Pennyfeather (*he reads from his paper*) presents an interpretive dance . . . a bit of culture entitled, "The Little Buds of Spring."

OPAL PENNYFEATHER. (*Enters from the wings. She is dressed in flowing robes with silk scarves fluttering from her arms and head and shoulders. She is barefooted and she executes a dance. She is supposed to be graceful and elegant; instead she is clumsy. She performs to the end, however, and there is a bit of applause. She bows and bows and throws kisses and finally exits.*)

MASTER OF CEREMONIES. (*claps, but his enthusiasm is dwindling*) I'm sure . . . (*looking at his paper*) the next person on the show needs no introduction. She is none other than Felicia Quimby, president of the Culture Club of Cucumber Center. Mrs. Quimby will deliver a dramatic reading from *Macbeth* by William Shakespeare. Mrs. Quimby . . .

FELICIA QUIMBY. (*She is the literary pillar of the town and she is aware of it. She is in a long formal gown with ropes of pearls around her neck. She fingers them delicately, comes to the center of the stage and takes a moment to "get in the mood." Then she delivers—and that's the word for it—Lady Macbeth's sleepwalking scene,* SCENE ONE, ACT FIVE. *It begins with "Yet here's a spot," and disregarding the speeches of the other characters continues as a soliloquy through "To bed, to bed, to bed." She substitutes "darned" for "damned" and omits the word "Hell." She bows with great dignity when she finishes and there is applause as she exits.*)

MASTER OF CEREMONIES. (*looks down at his paper*) You can't say we don't have variety here tonight, folks. Mr. Sam Tinker is next on the program with a group of barber shop melodies . . . Mr. Tinker. (MR. TINKER *does not enter. Again the* MANAGER *comes in. This time he whispers something to* PEABODY.) Well, I guess we won't have Mr. Tinker after all. It seems his wife just presented him with a bouncing boy and he's down at the hospital passing out cigars. Maybe next year. (*checks his list again*) Now you know, folks, there were a couple of other numbers here, but I see they were crossed off just before I came on. Cold feet, maybe? (*laughs*) We're running late anyhow. Be sure to vote for your favorite and drop your ballot in the barrel in the lobby. The winner'll be notified and will represent Cucumber Center at Grundy Springs next week, same night, same time. It's only a little drive over there, folks. You all come, now. (*He waves good-by and exits as the curtain closes.*)

SUGGESTIONS

The easiest thing about this variety show is that the performances don't have to be good. It doesn't matter what happens—forgotten lines, stage fright. The fellow with the hook can always pull the entertainer off the stage if things go too badly, and laughter is guaranteed.

You can add or subtract acts from the script as it stands here. You might have someone who can do magic tricks, a couple of good ones, perhaps, before a blooper. Or a very small musician who drags in a tuba or a bass fiddle. Whether he can play it or not is unimportant.

Dollie Dobbs might try a genuine vocal selection, preferably operatic, and sing enough of it for the audience to know she is terrible. The dance might have an added spark if there was off-stage music as an accompaniment, anything of your choosing. Could the juggler have real plates (if you can come by cracked ones that are going to be discarded anyhow) which fall and break? The manager might come on with a dust pan to clean up the pieces. And finally, should Shakespeare be above the interest of your actors, you can substitute something with which they are more familiar.

I suppose you could throw in a real talent if you had one, but it would be a little risky. The audience would have to know ahead of time that this was on the level. If Mary Jones can actually play Bach like a prodigy, you wouldn't want any funny business to upset her. Better to keep it all on a ridiculous basis.

Since you are giving the show a thirties background, put all the performers in clothes of that era except for the announcer, of course. He plays it straight.

IF YOU RECOGNIZE ME, DON'T ADMIT IT

CHARACTERS

ANNOUNCER
SCENE ONE, TEACHER AND STUDENTS
SCENE TWO, FATHER AND SON
SCENE THREE, CLERK IN SPORTING GOODS STORE AND CUSTOMER
SCENE FOUR, MOTHER AND CHILD
SCENE FIVE, GARAGE MECHANIC AND CUSTOMER
SCENE SIX, ACCIDENT VICTIM AND MOTORIST
THE HITCHHIKERS
SANTA CLAUS
SURFER
SKIER
CONVICT
SKIN DIVER
THE DEVIL

ANNOUNCER *enters from the left in front of the closed curtain.*

ANNOUNCER. Let's get right to the point. We would like to present for your entertainment a number of unlikely scenes. And just one word of advice. If you feel you bear any resemblance to the speakers you will hear, don't admit it.

(*As the* ANNOUNCER *exits, the curtain opens on* SCENE ONE. *It is a schoolroom.* STUDENTS *are at their desks. The* TEACHER *stands at the head of the class with a test paper in hand.*)

TEACHER. Now, if everyone is ready for the exam, we'll begin. Remember you may leave as soon as you complete the test, but there is no time limit. I will stay right here until everyone has finished. And one more thing. I want all of you to pass with top grades. If a problem stumps you, feel free to look at your neighbor's paper . . . (*pauses*) If you don't feel you can trust your neighbor, then simply open your books. At the end of Chapter Three you will find all the correct answers. (*Quick curtain.*)

(*The first hitchhiker,* SANTA CLAUS, *enters from the left in front of the closed curtain. He uses his thumb until he gets about midway across the stage and then lifts his sign:* SOUTH POLE. *As he exits, the curtain opens on* SCENE TWO. FATHER *is seated on the edge of his desk, and his* SON *stands before him.*)

FATHER. You just aren't getting enough money, son. I'm raising your allowance to twenty-five dollars a week . . . (*pauses*) retroactive from the first of last year. (*Quick curtain.*)

(*The second hitchhiker, the* SKIER, *enters from the left in front of the curtain. He waggles his thumb as he ambles across the stage. About halfway to the exit he lifts his sign,* MIAMI BEACH. *As he exits, the curtain opens on* SCENE THREE *which is laid in a sporting goods store. The* CLERK *stands with his hands on the shoulder of a young* CUSTOMER.)

CLERK. I know you told me you have no money . . . you're just browsing around, but we have a surprise for you. As the first person to come through our door this morning you receive a complimentary gift . . . (*pauses*) a ten-speed, racer bike. (*Quick curtain.*)

(*The third hitchhiker, the* SURFER, *enters from the left and when he gets midway across the stage lifts his sign:* DEATH VALLEY. *As he exits the curtain goes up on* SCENE FOUR. MOTHER *is speaking to her* CHILD.)

MOTHER. Of course you can stay up to watch the late, late movie. Help yourself if you want anything to eat. There's ice cream and soda pop in the refrigerator and a box of chocolates in the cupboard. (*turns to leave, pauses*) Oh yes, if you don't feel like getting up for school in the morning, I'll write an excuse. (*Quick curtain.*)

(*Fourth hitchhiker,* CONVICT, *enters in front of the curtain. He proceeds across the stage as the others before him. As he gets near the exit he lifts his sign:* SAN QUENTIN. *As he exits, the curtain opens on* SCENE FIVE. *A* GARAGE MECHANIC *is standing with a* CUSTOMER.)

MECHANIC. You bet your car's ready, sir. (*He takes a work order out of his pocket and checks it.*) Let's see, we put in a new pump, sealed off that leak in the radiator, relined the breaks, cleaned the spark plugs, and adjusted the carburetor. (*figures*) O.K. sir, that'll be three dollars and ten cents. (*pauses*) There's no charge at all for the labor. (*Quick curtain.*)

(*Fifth hitchhiker, the* SKIN DIVER *enters and plods his way across the stage in his flapping footgear. Shortly before he reaches the right exit he holds up his sign:* MT. EVEREST. *As he exits the curtain opens on* SCENE SIX. *A heavily bandaged* ACCIDENT VICTIM *speaks to the* MOTORIST.)

VICTIM. I know you didn't mean to go through the red light and hit me in the crosswalk. It was careless of me not to jump out of your way . . . (*pauses*) I wouldn't think of having you pay my hospital bills. (*Quick curtain.*)

(*The sixth hitchhiker, the* DEVIL *enters. He hops and dances his way across the stage waving his thumb. He exits, then pops back in to show his sign:* PARADISE.)

SUGGESTIONS

Since these individual scenes are short and complete within themselves, you can take certain ones out and add others as you wish. The possibilities are limitless, and even as you read this, ideas are probably bouncing around in your head—especially for situations that will have meaning for your particular audience. How about a woman applicant who says she doesn't expect as much pay as a man because she's not worth it, a school principal who extends the recess time and allows two hours for lunch, or an employer who announces a three-day work week with salary increases. Your selections will be governed, of course, by the kind of audience you have, young people, adults, or both.

As for the hitchhikers, again you can come up with any number of unlikely thumb artists who will get a laugh from the group you are entertaining.

You need very little in the way of props. The desk in the teacher scene can be kept on for Scenes Two and Three. Just whisk the student chairs out of the way. The number of students is up to you. You might have only three or four.

The scenes are almost like cartoons, with speeches like cartoon captions. They should move quickly, and since each one involves different players, not much time is needed between them.

In the scenes, incidentally, the lines help to identify the characters. However, the audience should be able to see that one actor is the father and the other the son, one the mother and the other the child. The garage mechanic might have coveralls and a grease-smudged face. Bandage the accident victim from head to toe and put him on crutches. The more bandages, the more laughs.

On the other hand, the costumes of the hitchhikers are all important. The players must be recognized instantly for what they are.

MRS. CLOPSADDLE PRESENTS CHRISTMAS

CHARACTERS

MRS. CLOPSADDLE, WHO DIRECTS THE SCHOOL OF ELOCUTION IN THE EARLY 1900's
PAUL, WHO RECITES A POEM
HENRIETTA, WHO HAS A CHRISTMAS RHYME
JOE, THE ANGEL
WILLIAM, WHO TELLS (ALMOST) A STORY
PETER, WHO SLEEPS
PHILLIP, WHO SINGS

MRS. CLOPSADDLE *sweeps onto the stage. She is overdressed, has a corsage of mistletoe and a sprig of holly in her hair.*

MRS. CLOPSADDLE. Welcome, welcome, welcome. The Clopsaddle School of Elocution presents its annual Christmas program. I am delighted that all of you could come. We won't waste time with idle talk, however, because our little people do get tired when the evening wears on. We will start at once and here is Paul Anderson with a little poem.

PAUL. (*marches in and recites like a robot, no expression, no gestures, no life.*)

At first I thought when I grew up I'd be a baseball star,
Or own a bank, or sail a ship to far off Zanzibar.

But when December rolled around, I changed my mind . . . because
I'd rather grow up big and fat and just be Santa Claus. (*He exits.*)

(MRS. CLOPSADDLE *leads the applause.* WILLIAM *starts to enter, but* MRS. CLOPSADDLE *waves him back.*)

MRS. CLOPSADDLE. No, William, not yet. It's not your turn. (*she turns to the audience*) Now little Henrietta Wilkins with a little-known Christmas rhyme.

HENRIETTA. (*Reluctant to come out of the wings, she is pushed from behind; she twists her handkerchief, bows and ducks her head bashfully.*)

Christmas is a-comin' and I can hardly wait.
I'm watchin' out for Santa Claus, if he isn't late.
I know he'll bring me lots of toys, and natcherly a tree.
I'm askin' for a dolly, too; I hope one asks for me.
We're all a-gettin' ready; even papa helps, you know.
While mama put up Christmas bells, he hung the mistletoe.

MRS. CLOPSADDLE. Thank you, Henrietta. (*to the audience*) Isn't she the picture of her mother? (HENRIETTA *doesn't leave.*) That's all, dear . . . thank you . . .

HENRIETTA. (*still doesn't leave; she bows again and starts her verse once more*) Christmas is a-comin' and I can hardly wait . . .

MRS. CLOPSADDLE. No, dear, you've finished . . . that's all now . . . (*She takes* HENRIETTA *and leads her to the exit. Then she comes back to her place and flutters her hands in confusion.*) Well, now where were we? (WILLIAM *tries to enter again.*) No, not yet, William. It's Joseph's time. Joseph Reedy, with a little recitation. I wager his mother won't recognize him. (JOE *emerges as an angel, but his white costume is dirty, one wing is almost off, and his halo is cocked over a very black eye.*) Oh, dear, I hardly recognize him myself.

JOE. (*speaks rapidly and keeps looking to the wings as though afraid someone is coming after him*) I'm the Christmas angel. I appeared to the shepherds soon after the Christ Child was born and said, "Do not be afraid. I bring you good news. In Bethlehem was born a Savior, Christ the Lord. You will find the baby lying in a manger."

(JOE *exits in the opposite direction from which he entered, all the time looking off-stage right.* WILLIAM *enters again.*)

MRS. CLOPSADDLE. All right, William. Yes, you can tell your story now. (*to the audience*) We made it up together. (*turns back to* WILLIAM) Didn't we, William?

WILLIAM. (*ignores the question*) Well, once upon a time there was this boy, see. He lived right here in this very town. He knew exactly what he wanted for Christmas. A real bow and arrow, a baseball glove, a real, and I mean *real,* hunting gun, a compass . . . (*He rattles off the list with determination, and* MRS. CLOPSADDLE *begins to show surprise.*)

MRS. CLOPSADDLE. That doesn't sound like the story we wrote, William.

WILLIAM. (*edges away from her toward the exit but continues*) It's kind of a real story. Bill was this guy's name. Sure, his list was pretty long, but he had a reason for it. The year before he asked for all these same things, and he didn't get any of them. You know what he got? Six pairs of stockings, a dictionary, winter rubbers, and a violin.

MRS. CLOPSADDLE. Oh my, William. I'm not sure that's a good Christmas story at all. Don't you remember *our* little boy didn't ask for anything . . .

WILLIAM. Not this kid. And if he doesn't get what he wants *this year* . . .

MRS. CLOPSADDLE. (*hustles him off-stage*) That will be all, William . . . that's enough . . . (*As she succeeds in pushing him off she returns to her place. She is very flustered.*) Such an imaginative child. That was quite a story. My goodness. Well, now . . . I think that brings us to Peter Holmes who will give us a recitation.

(MRS. CLOPSADDLE *looks off to the wings but* PETER *doesn't appear. She calls his name but still no* PETER. *Finally someone comes on to whisper a message.*)

MRS. CLOPSADDLE. I'm so sorry. I guess we waited a little too long for Peter. He has fallen asleep. We'll just have to go on to Phillip Stone who has a song for us.

(PHILLIP *enters, is given a pitch, and in a voice off key sings a Christmas song.* MRS. CLOPSADDLE *invites the audience to join in a final chorus and then calls the performers out to be introduced again.* PETER *is carried onto the stage. He is still sound asleep and stays so even through the applause.*)

SUGGESTIONS

This is something of a companion piece to *Mrs. Clopsaddle Presents Spring*. There, however, an announcer tells the audience where they are in time. You may prefer to do that, but costuming should be enough to set the stage. If Mrs. Clopsaddle comes out in one of those hobble skirts, you put the boys in knee pants, and you put the girls in cotton stockings and middie dresses and give them big ribbon bows to hold back their hair, everyone will get the idea.

As it stands the show will come off rather well, but you may have better ideas for the individual performers. Phillip's song should certainly be of your choosing. Do what you will.

PART V

THE SKETCH

THE SKETCH

. . . pick up your cue . . .

Perhaps you have started at the beginning of this book and moved along with it from the simplest show to the more difficult. If so, each member of your group has by this time been called or pushed or carried on to the stage at a given time, spoken lines perhaps, and retreated to the wings.

The thought of that lovely clatter of applause will keep you on your toes—success is intoxicating. However, you must now share the responsibility for that success, and the sketch or skit gives you the opportunity. Here we have a very short play with a bit of a plot, action, and lines for most of the actors to learn. But memory is more important than it has been before. You will depend on the others in the cast to enter and speak and exit when they are supposed to because you are going to enter or speak or exit on the cues they give you.

Of course, there should be a prompter. Even professional companies have someone in the wings ready to feed a line to the player who forgets. However, think positively. *No one will forget.* Keep your mind on the show and practice, practice, practice.

O.K. It's your turn.

IF THE RABBIT PICKETS, YOU'RE DOING SOMETHING WRONG

CHARACTERS

JOHNNY APPLESEED, THE NARRATOR

HOMER, THE GARDENER (FOUR STAGES OF HIS LIFE)

HIS MOTHER, WHO GOES FROM ADULTHOOD TO ANGELHOOD

THE RABBIT, A SCENE STEALER

THE OLD MAN

THE LADY IN THE AUDIENCE

HER CHILDREN, ANY NUMBER

As the show begins the auditorium is still lit and the curtain is closed. JOHNNY *enters from the rear and comes down the aisle to the stage. He talks as he walks.*

JOHNNY. Apple seeds! Get your apple seeds! Right here. Plant yourself a tree. Apple seeds . . . nice fresh apple seeds, itchin' to grow. (*He pauses now and then to nod to members of the audience.*) Think of those big red apples. And think of the applesauce and the apple pies and the apple dumplings. Isn't your mouth just watering for all that goodness? But you can't have the fruit unless you plant the tree. (*He stops to speak to the* WOMAN *with all the children.*) Hello there, lady, are all these children yours? Well, you've no time for planting, I can see that. You'd better take an apple. (*He gives her an apple and ambles on.*) Apple seeds! Apple seeds! (*He *moves on up to the stage. There is an* OLD MAN *sitting on the floor at the side in front of the closed curtain. He has a short beard and a placard around his neck which reads:* OLD. *He seems to be unaware of what's going on as* JOHNNY *continues.*) Well, folks, I guess I don't need an introduction. Johnny's the name. Johnny Appleseed they call me, and I know you've heard how I traveled around the country planting apple seeds. But that's not why I'm here now. No siree! I've got a story to tell. You know I've talked to a good many folks in my travels, and I've met a lot of gardeners. But out of the whole lot there was only one fellow who worried me. Homer Throttlebottle. Yes siree! Homer had me worried for a good long time.

(*Curtain opens and* HOMER, *in short pants and wearing a big gardener's apron, stands at the right with his* MOTHER, *who is dressed in old-fashioned clothes and wears a sunbonnet.*)

JOHNNY. (*continuing*) Homer was just a little fellow when he first decided he wanted a garden. That's his maw there with him.

MOTHER. (*adjusting an old straw hat on* HOMER'*s head*) Keep your head covered from the sun now, Homer.

HOMER. I will, mama.

MOTHER. And don't get yourself too dirty, Homer. (*She puts seed packets in his apron pockets.*)

HOMER. I won't, mama.

MOTHER. And plant us a nice garden, Homer.

HOMER. I will, mama. (MOTHER *exits and* HOMER *picks up a rake and hoe and moves to the center of the stage.*)

JOHNNY. Oh, Homer planned a fine garden, all right. Peas and beans and carrots . . . a lot of carrots, because Homer liked carrots. And lettuce, too. (HOMER *works while* JOHNNY *talks, suiting the actions to the words*) He worked like a beaver. And when he was finished he wiped his brow. There was his garden with all the little placards set up to tell him where things were. Peas and beans and lettuce and carrots.

THE OLD MAN. (*seems to come to life to speak*) 'Tain't no use, son. 'Twon't sprout nohow. (HOMER *ignores the* OLD MAN *and goes off right.*)

JOHNNY. I suppose you're wondering who that fellow is. Well, sir, he's just an old timer who lives across the road from Homer. He don't do a thing 'cept just sit. But Homer should have heeded his words. 'Cause now Homer, he watered that garden, (HOMER *enters and works*) and he hoed it, and he watched it, but just like that old timer said, it warn't no use. Nothin' grew. (HOMER *goes off dejected.*) Nothin', that is, except Homer. (JOHNNY *munches on the apple he has been holding while the* RABBIT *comes in, sniffs around the garden and goes out.*) But Homer wasn't easily discouraged. It wasn't long before he decided to try again. He was a little bigger now and he thought he was wiser.

(*As* JOHNNY *is talking the* OLD MAN *puts on a longer beard and changes his placard. It now reads:* OLDER. HOMER *appears at the right as before with his* MOTHER. *He is no longer dressed as a child. He wears jeans but still has the big apron. His* MOTHER *is a little stooped with the years.*)

MOTHER. Keep your head covered from the sun now, Homer. (*She puts the straw hat on him as before.*)

HOMER. I will, mama.

MOTHER. And don't get yourself too dirty, Homer.

HOMER. I won't, mama.

MOTHER. And plant us a nice garden, Homer. (*She puts seeds in his apron.*)

HOMER. I will, mama. (MOTHER *exits and* HOMER *picks up the hoe and works.*)

JOHNNY. Oh, Homer planned a fine garden all right. Peas and beans and carrots . . . a lot of carrots, because Homer liked carrots. And lettuce too. (HOMER *works while* JOHNNY *talks, suiting the actions to the words*) He worked like a beaver. And when he was finished he wiped his brow. There was his garden with all the little placards set up to tell him where things were. Peas and beans and lettuce and carrots.

THE OLD MAN. (*comes to life again*) 'Tain't no use, son. 'Twon't sprout nohow. (HOMER *ignores the* OLD MAN *and goes off right.*)

JOHNNY. Well, now Homer he watered that garden (HOMER *enters and works*) and he hoed it, and he watched it. But just like that old timer said, it warn't no use. (*Exit* HOMER *dejectedly.*) Nothin' grew. Nothin', that is, except Homer. (JOHNNY *munches on his apple while the* RABBIT *comes in, sniffs around the garden, and goes out.*) Now the years slipped by, and Homer grew to be a man. His maw had left him and gone to heaven, but she still watches over him as he gathers his tools and starts out to dig his garden . . . (*The* OLD MAN *puts on a longer beard and replaces the placard around his neck to one which reads:* VERY, VERY, OLD. HOMER *appears at the right and his* MOTHER, *an angel now with wings but with the same dress and sunbonnet, sort of hovers beside him.*) There were the same stakes . . . the peas and the beans and the carrots . . . no, let's see now, Homer got pretty tired of carrots. Instead of carrots it looks like he planned on spinach . . . and lettuce, of course. And he worked like a beaver. And when he was finished he wiped his brow.

THE OLD MAN. 'Tain't no use, son. 'Twon't sprout nohow.

(HOMER *ignores the* OLD MAN *and exits.*)

JOHNNY. Well, sir, Homer he watered and hoed that garden. And he watched it. But just like the old timer said, it warn't no use. Nothin' grew. Not even Homer anymore. (HOMER, *who has been working, exits in despair.* JOHNNY *eats his apple and the* RABBIT *comes in with a picket sign:* THIS GARDEN UNFAIR TO A HARE.) Now the years went by again. (*The* OLD MAN *changes his placard once more to* ANCIENT *and his beard to one which curls on the floor beside him, and* HOMER *appears at the right.*) Poor old Homer. He is stooped now and walks with a cane, but his angel maw still watches over him. (MOTHER *appears and shakes her head as* HOMER *starts off with his tools and with his big gardener's apron still tied around him.*) Well, it was the same old thing. The peas and the beans and the spinach, and the lettuce too. It was pretty hard for Homer to bend over these days, but he worked like a beaver. And when he finished he wiped his brow.

THE OLD MAN. 'Tain't no use son. 'Twon't grow nohow. (HOMER *ignores him and exits.*)

JOHNNY. Well, sir, Homer watered that garden (HOMER *comes in and works*) and he hoed it, and he watched it. But just like that old fellow said, 'twarn't no use. Nothin' grew. And now Homer had had about all he could take. Homer Throttlebottle had planted his last garden. It was the saddest thing I ever saw.

(HOMER *takes off his apron and discards it and then exits sadly.*)

THE OLD MAN. (*Drags himself to his feet and hobbles to center stage with the aid of a crooked stick. He picks up the apron, turns it upside down and all the seed packets fall to the floor*) I told the boy. I told him it warn't no use. All these years he's been forgettin' the seeds. (*Quick curtain.*)

JOHNNY. Well, that's the end of my story. And I suppose there's a lesson here. Keep your mind on what you're doing . . . and heed the old timers. (*He ambles down from the stage and exits as he came, handing out seed packets.*) Apple seeds! Apple seeds! Get your apple seeds.

SUGGESTIONS

This sketch can be performed on a bare stage. Only a bit of costuming and a few hand props will be needed. For Johnny Appleseed a sauce pan hat, boots, and a knapsack. He can have a real apple to eat (if he can talk around it) and carry one for the lady as well.

Homer will change his clothes to fit his age as indicated in the script, but the apron is essential. Any kind that has a large pocket will do. Garden tools will add a touch of realism, and the placards naming the vegetables should be large enough to be seen from the audience. If you can't get real seed packets, use envelopes. Color them with crayon a bit and fill them with sand or pebbles, just so they have some weight.

Mama should have a long old-fashioned dress and a sunbonnet if possible—otherwise a shawl for her head. Wings can be made of cardboard or wire covered with muslin. They need only suggest the idea.

If you can't find a rabbit costume left over from Halloween, you can make a mask out of cloth and ears out of wire. You might use a gray sweat suit and attach a cotton tail. Just be sure the audience knows it's a rabbit even if you have to hang a sign around his neck.

The old timer's beard can be made of curled newspaper strips, each one longer than the last. His signs telling his age are the only other props he needs.

The lady in the audience can dress in clothes of the day, but you might have her wearing a hat to set her apart.

BETTER LUCK TOMORROW, MR. WASHINGTON

CHARACTERS

THE GUIDE

THE TOURISTS, ANY NUMBER

MARTHA

GEORGE

The scene is laid in the sitting room of Tuckaway Inn in Virginia. It is decorated in the style of the eighteenth century, apparently preserved as it was at that time. The room is roped off and there is a sign propped up at the right: GEORGE WASHINGTON SLEPT HERE. *As the curtain opens the* GUIDE *enters followed by the* TOURISTS *who file by along the rope.*

GUIDE. (*taking a position at the left of the stage*) As you can see, this is an historic place. This little inn along with hundreds like it has become endeared to all Americans, because these very rooms were once occupied on a memorable night back in the eighteenth century by George and Martha Washington. The sleeping quarters are off to the left. You will note the sign. Now I don't mean to tear down the sentiment that accompanies such points of interest, but I happen to be in possession of certain facts. My great-great-great-great-grandmother (*he pauses to count on his fingers*) I guess that's enough greats . . . was a chambermaid in this particular establishment and was inclined to listen at doors. In all fairness I must point out the unreliableness of signs, because this is what actually happened. Let us assume that it is the morning of February 22, 1775. There comes Martha from the bedroom.

MARTHA. (*enters and settles herself in a comfortable chair as she takes up her knitting*) My, but I did sleep well.

GEORGE. (*enters, yawning and grumbling*) Did you say something to me?

MARTHA. Only that I slept well . . . and good morning to you, Mr. Washington.

GEORGE. I can't see anything good about it.

MARTHA. Why it's your birthday, and I'm sure you had a good, sound sleep.

GEORGE. Confound it, Martha, I didn't sleep a wink. The bed was atrocious. It had great lumps in it. I think they put the feathers in without removing them from the chickens. And not half enough quilts for a cold night. I'm frozen.

MARTHA. Oh, George, I'm so sorry. Would you like me to send for a cup of tea?

GEORGE. Bother the tea . . . what I need is sleep. Just when I was ready to drop off in complete exhaustion, the roosters started to crow.

MARTHA. Well, I slept like a log. I feel wonderfully refreshed.

GEORGE. That doesn't do me any good. How can I be expected to cross the Delaware or endure a winter at Valley Forge or defeat the British at all if I don't get any sleep. I'll be lucky if I even live to be president of this great nation.

MARTHA. All right, George. We'll just pack up and leave here at once. Perhaps tonight we can find an inn with a bed that pleases you. (MARTHA *gets up and gathers up her knitting.*)

GEORGE. I don't care if it's a haystack. This shouldn't happen to the father of one's country. And on his birthday, too. (*He grumbles to himself as they exit.*)

GUIDE. And so you see the sign is wrong. Someday someone will correct the error. Now if you'll just step this way. (*As the group files past the roped off area and exits, the last* TOURIST *slips back in and crosses out* GEORGE *on the sign and writes* MARTHA *above it as the curtain closes.*)

SUGGESTIONS

Although the scene indicates a colonial sitting room, it isn't necessary at all. You might even add a touch of humor by having an almost bare stage, only a rocker or armchair for Martha, and one of the tourists commenting about the lack of furniture. The guide might reply, "Nobody ever said Tuckaway Inn was a fancy place."

The more important thing is to provide some kind of costume for Martha—a full-skirted dress and a ruffled morning cap. As for George, try to find a nightshirt and make a nightcap out of an old undershirt. It should be floppy and with a tassel on the end.

The tourists will wear clothes of the day, and the guide should have some kind of uniform jacket and a cap to set him apart.

Incidentally, if some of the tourists want lines, break up the guide's long speech by having people ask questions or make comments. "Where's the bedroom?" "What kind of facts?" "I listen at doors too."

APPLES FOR SALE

CHARACTERS

THE POOR LITTLE OLD LADY
THE POOR LITTLE GIRL
THE RICH LITTLE OLD LADY
FATE

As the curtain rises the POOR LITTLE OLD LADY *enters, dressed in ragged clothes, a shawl over her head, and a basket of apples in her arms.*

POOR LITTLE OLD LADY. (*speaking to the audience*) Apples . . . big, red, shiny apples . . . ten cents. Won't somebody please buy my apples? I am a poor little old lady, and I come here day after day selling big, red, shiny, apples. But nobody ever buys my big, red, shiny, apples, and every night I go home and have applesauce for dinner. I hate applesauce.

POOR LITTLE GIRL. (*enters and speaks to the audience*) I am a poor little girl, and I pass here day after day wishing I could buy a big, red, shiny, apple from that poor little old lady. But I never can buy a big, red, shiny, apple because they cost ten cents, and I don't ever have ten cents. I get so hungry for apples. (*Exits.*)

RICH LITTLE OLD LADY. (*enters and speaks to the audience*) I am a very rich little old lady, and I pass here day after day wishing somebody would buy that poor little old lady's apples. I'm getting sick and tired of hearing her call "Apples . . . big, red, shiny, apples . . . ten cents." I don't like apples. I don't even like apple pie, not even with ice cream. Or cheese either. (*Exits.*)

FATE. (*Enters dressed in long flowing robes and, speaking in a monotone, she addresses the audience.*) I am fate, and I stand over here day after day watching that poor little old lady and that poor little girl and that rich little old lady. I know that sooner or later something is going to happen. I don't dare go home, because if something does happen I will be responsible. (*She turns around to reveal a placard on her back which says* TIME ELAPSES, *then she faces the audience again.*)

RICH LITTLE OLD LADY. (*enters and speaks as before*) Well, sooner or later has arrived, and I have decided that I am going to buy all of the little old lady's apples even if I don't like them. I'll give them to that little girl.

POOR LITTLE GIRL. (*enters*) Well, sooner or later has arrived, and even though I still don't have ten cents I am going to get that little old lady's apples, because that rich little old lady is going to buy them and give them to me. You heard her, didn't you?

POOR LITTLE OLD LADY. (*enters with her basket, but the apples are gone and in their place are violets*) Well, sooner or later has arrived, and I decided to do something about it. I just turned in all my apples and bought violets instead. Violets! Violets! Ten cents a bunch . . .

POOR LITTLE GIRL. I'm certainly not hungry for violets. I guess I'll go home. (*She exits.*)

RICH LITTLE OLD LADY. Well, I like violets less than I like apples. I'm allergic to violets. They give me goose bumps and make me sneeze. (*She sneezes.*) I guess I'll go home too. (*Exits.*)

FATE. And the point of this story is that sometimes you just can't win. That's fate. I guess I can go home now too. (*Exits.*)

POOR LITTLE OLD LADY. (*remains alone on the stage looking more forlorn than ever*) Violets! Violets! Won't somebody please buy my violets? Please. I hope somebody buys my violets. They make very poor sauce. (*Quick curtain.*)

Suggestions

There is so little needed to make this skit effective. A curtain is indicated, but the poor little old lady could simply deliver her punch line to the audience and then exit still calling out her wares: "Violets! Violets! Won't somebody buy my violets?"

Costumes are easy and are suggested in the script. By all means exaggerate both the rags and the riches. Tatters and patches for the poor little old lady and the girl, and perhaps furs and jewelry for the wealthy one.

Props are few in number and not difficult to provide: a basket, apples, violets. And of course you can change the flower if it's more convenient: daisies, geraniums, even petunias, either real or artificial.

TURKEYS TAKE A DIM VIEW OF THANKSGIVING

CHARACTERS

BETSY, AN ORDINARY LITTLE GIRL
HER MOTHER
FIRST TURKEY
SECOND TURKEY
THE BIG GOBBLER

SCENE ONE—IN BETSY'S HOME
SCENE TWO—IN TURKEYLAND
SCENE THREE—BACK IN BETSY'S HOME

As SCENE ONE *opens* BETSY *enters with school books. Her* MOTHER *is seated in a chair, sewing.*

BETSY. (*with little enthusiasm*) Guess what? I have to tell my class the story of the first Thanksgiving.

MOTHER. That should be interesting. Do you want to practice on me?

BETSY. I don't even know what to say yet.

MOTHER. Maybe I can help. (*She puts aside her sewing and goes to look for a particular book on the shelf.*)

BETSY. Oh, I've already looked up a few facts. The pilgrims, one hundred and two of them, landed in Massachusetts in 1620.

(*In the meantime* MOTHER *has found the book and the reference.*)

MOTHER. Yes, here is the story. (*She reads.*) "It was already late in the year and cold, and many of them died that first winter. When spring came those who remained planted crops."

BETSY. Did they have seed?

MOTHER. (*looking up from the book*) Oh yes, they brought some with them from the Old World, and the Indians gave them corn and taught them how to plow the land. (*Reads again.*) "The first harvest was bountiful, and in gratitude to God and to show friendliness to the Indians Governor Bradford issued an invitation to Chief Massasoit and his braves to a Thanksgiving feast which should last from Thursday morning until Saturday night. That was in October, 1621."

BETSY. Did the Indians like the feast?

MOTHER. I'm sure they did. Governor Bradford sent out his best riflemen to bring in wild turkeys. The women made corn pudding . . .

BETSY. (*interrupting*) Did they have pumpkin pie?

MOTHER. Well, they had pumpkin, but they probably used it as a vegetable, maybe cooking it in its own shell.

BETSY. I'm not sure I'd like that.

MOTHER. Well, it was a long time before Thanksgiving became the holiday we know now. Here, you read the book. You'll find out all about it.

BETSY. I hope there isn't too much to tell. I'll never remember.

MOTHER. You can pick out just what you want. I'd better get started on our dinner. I'll check back a little later to see what you've found. (*She exits.*)

BETSY. (*curls up in the chair with the book, thumbing through the pages and repeating names to herself*) The part I like best is about the plump turkeys. I makes me hungry just to read about them. And sleepy too, just as though I'd eaten a big Thanksgiving dinner myself. (BETSY *nods and falls asleep as two* TURKEYS *enter from the left. At first they do not see* BETSY.)

FIRST TURKEY. Do you realize that it is almost Thanksgiving Day again?

SECOND TURKEY. Thanksgiving! I don't know what there is for us to be thankful for. Trouble Day is a better name for it.

FIRST TURKEY. The Big Gobbler doesn't do very much to protect us, either. All he can suggest is to keep very thin, so that the people won't want us.

SECOND TURKEY. And that isn't much of a suggestion. I get mighty hungry.

FIRST TURKEY. (*seeing* BETSY) Say, do you see what I see? Isn't that a people?

SECOND TURKEY. It sure is, and I have an idea. (*whispers to his friend*)

FIRST TURKEY. But isn't a people too big for us to handle?

SECOND TURKEY. Not when they're asleep. Come on. (*They tie* BETSY *up and carry her off right.*)

(*The curtain closes and opens again at once on* SCENE TWO *which is in Turkeyland at the general headquarters of the* BIG GOBBLER. *He is sitting at a desk broadcasting his Thanksgiving message to his fellow birds.*)

BIG GOBBLER. I can only repeat . . . Thanksgiving Day is upon us once again. I hearby declare Turkeydom to be in a state of emergency. If any wise bird has an idea please come forward before it is too late. This is general headquarters . . . the Big Gobbler signing off.

(*The two* TURKEYS *enter with* BETSY.)

BIG GOBBLER. Well, what have we here?

FIRST TURKEY. We have a very interesting prisoner, sir . . . a people.

BIG GOBBLER. How did you happen to catch her? Surely she wasn't sleeping.

SECOND TURKEY. She certainly was, sir. Very careless of her.

FIRST TURKEY. We'd like to bring her to trial, sir.

BIG GOBBLER. Right away . . . right away. There is no time to lose. I may not be here by the end of the day. Those two families down by the lake have been watching me closely. Now then . . . (*to* BETSY) have you anything to say for yourself, people?

BETSY. I'm a girl, and I think this is very unfair.

BIG GOBBLER. Unfair, unfair, she says. Let me ask you one question. What did you have for Thanksgiving dinner last year?

BETSY. Why, turkey, of course, and dressing and cranberries and . . .

FIRST TURKEY. See. She admits it. Off with her head.

BIG GOBBLER. And what did you have the year before?

BETSY. Why, the same thing. We always have the regular Thanksgiving dinner . . . like everybody else. It's a tradition.

SECOND TURKEY. If that isn't enough evidence I'll turn in my wattle. Off with her head! Off with her head! I'll get the axe.

BIG GOBBLER. We could pen her up for awhile first. Let her think about her crime. Then we could punish her.

FIRST TURKEY. I say do it now.

BIG GOBBLER. I have another idea. Maybe we can make a deal. (*to* BETSY) If you promise to see to it that *no one* has turkey on his table this year we might let you go.

BETSY. I can't promise that. Some people already have their turkeys.

BIG GOBBLER. Well, then things look bad for you. There's nothing I can do. Get the axe. (*He motions* SECOND TURKEY *to leave.*)

BETSY. (*as* SECOND TURKEY *exits*) No! No! You can't do that. Help! Help!

(SECOND TURKEY *returns with the axe and moves toward her.*)

BIG GOBBLER. It's what you do to us, you know. An eye for an eye and a head for a head.

BETSY. No! Help! Mother! (*She runs offstage with the* TURKEYS *after her as the curtain falls.*)

(SCENE THREE *is the same as* SCENE ONE. BETSY *is still asleep in the chair.*)

BETSY. (*who is still dreaming*) Help! Help! Mother, don't let them do it.

MOTHER. (*enters from the right*) Don't let who do what, for goodness sake? What on earth is the matter?

BETSY. (*wakes up and rubs her eyes*) Oh, dear, I must have been dreaming. But I can't remember what . . .

MOTHER. And I thought you were working on your story. Do you know what you're going to say about the first Thanksgiving?

BETSY. Oh yes, I know exactly what I'm going to say. I'm going to tell about Governor Bradford and Chief Massasoit and about the riflemen going out to get turkeys . . . Oh no! Now I remember what I was dreaming. (*pauses*) Mother, will you do me a favor?

MOTHER. Certainly, if I can. What is it?

BETSY. This Thanksgiving could we have hamburgers instead of turkey?

MOTHER. I thought turkey was your favorite food. (*laughs*) But if you want hamburgers . . .

(*There is a loud "moo" from offstage.*)

BETSY. (*who heard it*) By the way, what are hamburgers made from?

MOTHER. Beef . . . why? (*There is a louder "moo."*)

BETSY. Oh no, not again. I guess I'll just have to settle for cheese sandwiches. (*Quick curtain.*)

SUGGESTIONS

This skit needs only a few props—a chair for Betsy to curl up in, some kind of a book shelf, books, a table and chair for the Big Gobbler, and, of course, the axe.

The turkeys will be a challenge to the costume maker. Still, you can come up with a bit of magic with a few brown paper sacks. Large ones can be split and colored, with the edges clipped to resemble wings and fastened over the players' arms. Similarly, smaller sacks can be made into head pieces; and don't forget the red wattles. It is only necessary to suggest. The audience will go along with you.

Incidentally, if you want to get more of the Thanksgiving story in, the mother might read the full account, but be sure she is interrupted often by questions from Betsy. You are giving a play, not a history lesson. You don't want to bore anyone.

YOU CAN'T BLAME WOMEN FOR COMING OUT OF THE KITCHEN

Characters

ANNOUNCER

MR.

MRS.

BARON BARKO

The curtain is closed as the ANNOUNCER *enters and stands at the left side of the stage.*

ANNOUNCER. Do you want to know why the women's liberation movement really started? Well, just watch our little play, and I think you'll agree that you can't blame women for coming out of the kitchen.

(*Curtain opens on the first scene. It is morning in the breakfast room of a suburban home. There is a table plus a couple of chairs at left center. A television stands at the back a bit to the right, and a calendar hangs on the wall. It is one of those calendars with the date in large figures, one to a page. The year is not important or even the day as long as the date can be seen clearly.* MRS. *enters from the left. She is dressed in robe and slippers and has a curler cap on her head. She yawns, stretches, tears a page off the calendar and exits out through the kitchen right to get the paper. She returns with it, opens it up, and puts it on the table. As she goes off to the kitchen to get the coffeepot and cups,* MR. *enters from the left, strides to the table, opens out the paper, and begins to read.* MRS. *puts coffee down in front of him. He drinks, gets up to leave, accepts the briefcase from* MRS., *and exits left without ever taking his eyes off the paper.* MRS. *turns on the television and then sits down at the table and pours a cup of coffee for herself. The television comes to life and* BARON BARKO *appears.*)

BARON BARKO. Good morning girls. This is your friendly counselor, Baron Barko speaking. And how is your marriage today? Do you sparkle? Do you shine? Did your husband look fondly at you over the breakfast table? And did he kiss you affectionately as he left for work? No? Then take a good look at yourself. Are you sitting there in your bathrobe and your slippers? Are you hiding you hair beneath a cap? You are? For shame. And do you always look like that?

(MRS. *turns off the television and exits with a determined step as the curtain closes.*)

ANNOUNCER. No need to say anything here . . . only to indicate the passage of time. Nine o'clock, ten o'clock, noon, three, six, night. (*he pantomimes sleep*) Morning. (*he stretches*)

(SCENE TWO—*same as before except that* MRS. *enters dressed in an attractive housecoat, her hair combed, and carrying a pair of shoes to replace the slippers of the morning before. She puts these on, tears off the calendar date, and goes through the same routine as before.* MR. *reacts exactly as he did on the previous day. After he leaves,* MRS. *turns on the television.* BARON BARKO *appears again.*)

BARON BARKO. And how is your marriage *today?* Did your husband . . . (MRS. *snaps the television off in disgust and exits. Curtain closes.*)

ANNOUNCER. You're getting the idea. Time goes by rather quickly. It is now the third morning. Mrs. is a little earlier today. There are a few preparations she wants to make before her husband comes down.

(SCENE THREE—*same as before except that* MRS. *enters in a short dinner dress. She puts on long sparkling earrings and a necklace before she tears the page off the calendar. She has also carried a pair of high-heeled shoes in with her and she sits down to the table to slip them on. Finally she sweeps her hair on top of her head and tucks a brilliant comb in it before she goes through the rest of the actions of the last two scenes. This time when* MR. *exits, after having followed his usual procedure,* MRS. *just stands there in frustration. Then she turns on the television. When* BARON BARKO *appears she doesn't wait for him to speak . . . she just slaps his face and the curtain closes quickly.*)

ANNOUNCER. We could stop right here. Don't you think we've made a point? But just wait. Things get worse . . . because on the fourth morning . . .

(SCENE FOUR—*still the same, but* MRS. *enters looking sloppier than she did in* SCENE ONE. *She is in the old bathrobe and slippers, the curler cap is back on her head, and she yawns and scratches as she goes through the customary routine. When she goes to get the paper, she comes back empty-handed. It isn't there.* MR. *enters and goes to the table as* MRS. *exits for the coffee.*)

MR. (*shouts to her*) Where's the paper?

MRS. (*from offstage*) Didn't come.

MR. (*still shouting*) That's a fine thing. Did you call them?

MRS. Not yet. (*She reenters and puts the coffee in front of him.*) Here's your coffee.

MR. (*seeing her for the first time*) Good grief! (*He looks her over from head to foot very slowly.*) Do you *always* look like that? (*Quick curtain.*)

SUGGESTIONS

The small props are not difficult here: the calendar, briefcase, coffeepot, cups, and the paper. The table and chairs should also be no problem. The television will be your only challenge. You might use a large packing carton and fashion doors for it. It is turned on, and then when the doors are opened there is Barko, who, incidentally, should be mustached and self-assured. Another solution would be to have the television at the back against a curtain that could be draped around it. Barko could then come and go unseen behind the curtain. If you think it would be simpler, you might have a radio instead. Barko can be an offstage voice then, and after the dinner dress scene the wife can chuck the radio in a wastebasket.

The role of Mrs. will be the most fun and a wonderful opportunity for a bit of acting. There isn't much time for costume changes, but the clothes can simply be layered on—the sleeveless mini-skirted dinner dress underneath the housecoat which is underneath the robe. The cap can cover the first hair style. You can have someone in the wings to help speed things up.

You'll be pressed for time between Scenes Two and Three, but the script calls for the jewelry and the shoes to be put on, on stage. Also the change of hair style is made as the audience watches. You might even want to allow time for the wife to apply heavy eye shadow and false eyelashes. For the final scene, the make-up doesn't have to be taken off. Just smear it up a little as though she neglected everything the night before. One eyelash might be hanging. Exaggeration is the key. Why not have the wife spray perfume on herself and all around the room on the third morning and maybe put flowers on the table? Better yet, let her hold a rose in her teeth.

A business suit will be fine for the husband. He will get a chance to act too, because he must be putting on his coat and fussing with his tie as he enters so that he never looks at anything around him, especially his wife.

DON'T FALL ASLEEP, COACH, YOU MIGHT POSSIBLY DREAM

CHARACTERS

ANNOUNCER

COACH

JIM, HIS ASSISTANT

KELLY, THE CAPTAIN OF THE TEAM

BENSON, BOLTON, AND BEGGS, THREE OF THE LINEMEN

WILLIAMS AND WALSH, TACKLES

ANNOUNCER. (*stepping out in front of the closed curtain*) I don't have to tell anybody that we're in the football season. Some of you may battle the crowds to see your favorites play, whether they are high school, college, or pro teams. Others may huddle before a wide screen TV or listen with eager ear to the radio broadcasts. You probably have your pet quarterback or end or tackle. Certainly all attention is on the players. But at this time we'd like to consider the coaches. They have a lot of worries, and it is with great understanding that we take you to the office of the head coach at Dooley Prep as we present a little play entitled, *Don't Fall Asleep, Coach, You Might Possibly Dream.*

(*The curtain opens. The* COACH *is seated at his desk with his chin in his hands. He looks up as his* ASSISTANT *enters.*)

COACH. Hi, Jim. Come on in. We've got a few things to talk about.

ASSISTANT. The line was in good shape yesterday, Coach. It's a powerful team.

COACH. We've got some big fellows, all right, but we've got some speed too. (*phone rings and the* COACH *answers*) Hello. Oh, Kelly, yes, this is the coach. What's the trouble . . . (*he listens for a moment*) Well, get down here as fast as you can . . .

(*The* COACH *hangs up and almost immediately there is a knock at the door.*)

ASSISTANT. You're right about the speed, sir.

COACH. Come in.

(KELLY *doesn't enter, but he pokes his head in.*)

KELLY. (*out of breath and very excited*) Something terrible has happened.

COACH. Somebody sick?

KELLY. Worse than that, coach.

COACH. Craig break his leg again?

KELLY. I wish that was all it was, sir.

COACH. You mean he broke both legs?

KELLY. No, I mean it's not that . . .

COACH. Well, what then?

KELLY. Well, you know it rained last night, sir, and we got caught in it, and well, I just can't say it, sir. You'll have to see for yourself.

COACH. Stop stammering and get in here and tell me what this is all about.

(KELLY *comes on stage. The sleeves of his football jersey come well over his hands, and the pants are down to his ankles.*)

COACH and ASSISTANT together. Oh, no! You've shrunk.

KELLY. You know how it can rain, Coach.

COACH. Did this happen to any of the others?

KELLY. I'm afraid so, sir. Benton and Bolton and Beggs are outside.

(*He motions off-stage and the three enter. All of their uniforms are too big for them.*)

COACH. It can't have happened to everybody. Where're Walsh and Williams? They both weigh well over two hundred pounds. What about them?

KELLY. Almost the worst of all, sir. Here they are now.

(*The two enter. They are literally lost in their uniforms and their helmets are way down over their eyes. The* COACH *crumples at the table and sobs.*)

ASSISTANT. I know I shouldn't ask this, but what about Craig? He only weighed a hundred and fifty-eight.

KELLY. I'll get him, sir, but you'd better sit down too.

(KELLY *exits as the* ASSISTANT *takes a chair. The* COACH *sobs louder.* KELLY *comes back in almost at once. He holds a water bucket with a football helmet floating on top.*)

KELLY. This is what's left of him, sir. Craig just dissolved completely. And we're not just sure how much of this is Craig.

(*The* ASSISTANT *joins the* COACH *in tears as the curtain closes.*)

SUGGESTIONS

You really need full-sized football uniforms to make this come off—the high school coach might cooperate. Maybe it could be a plug for the local team and you could use real players' names. I suppose you might make do with extra large T-shirts or sweat shirts, but it won't be as effective.

Naturally you'll use the smallest boys available for

Walsh and Williams and the biggest ones for the coach and his assistant.

The rain or lack of it in your area or in the current season can dictate changes in the lines for more humor.

SURPRISE

(A classroom skit for the first of April)

CHARACTERS

ONE, TWO, THREE, AND FIVE, MEMBERS OF THE CLASS
FOUR, THE MESSENGER
THE REST OF THE STUDENTS (ACTUALLY THE AUDIENCE)

Those who are going to take part in the skit, except for the MESSENGER, *are planted about the room. Since the presentation is supposed to take place in the actual classroom (with the approval of the teacher of course) the speakers can simply remain in their own seats until otherwise directed. The lines are most effective when delivered in a syncopated rhythm.*

ONE.

There's a knock at the classroom door;
I'll go see what the knocking's for. (*Leaves his place and goes to the door.*)

TWO. (*shouts from his place*)

Maybe it's the principal come to say,
"All go home . . . have a holiday."

THREE. (*from his place*) Fine chance!

(ONE *opens the door to* FOUR *who has been standing outside waiting for his entrance.*)

FOUR.

Special delivery. I've a letter here
For the entire room. That much is clear.

THREE. (*quickly getting up from his place and going to the front*)

I can take it . . . let me sign. (*he does so as* ONE *opens the letter*)
There you are on the dotted line.

ONE. (*still holding the letter he addresses* FOUR)

Wait a minute. I may be dense,
But this crazy thing doesn't make any sense.
(THREE *takes the paper to read;* ONE *speaks to* FOUR *again*)
Better stick around if you don't mind.
We may need help. It's a code of some kind.

FOUR.

I'll be glad to stay, but I'm not much good
When it comes to riddles . . . (*points to his head*) . . . it's made of wood.

ONE.

Is there anyone here who can help us now?
We ought to get this message, but we don't know how.

FIVE. (*from his place*)

I'd write it on the board if I were you.
Then maybe someone will find a clue.

(*As* ONE *writes,* TWO *calls the letters, accenting them as indicated.*)

TWO.

L̓OO ÓFO L̓IOŔ (*pause*) ṔÓÁ
Sounds like a chant for a voodoo day.

FIVE.

Too many Os . . . why don't you take out
Every third letter and see how you make out.

ONE. (*does as suggested, saying at the same time*)
An O and an O and an O and an O
Does it do any good? I wouldn't know.

THREE. (*who has been watching from the sidelines*)
Of course, it's clear now, don't you see?
Give me the chalk; I have the key.

ONE. (*as he gives the chalk to* THREE)
Take it . . . I'm sorry I answered the door.
I'm more confused now than I was before.

TWO. (*reads the message as it now stands without the extra Os*)
Looflirpa! Looflirpa! What gibberish is that?
If you say it's English, I'll eat my hat.

THREE.

Hold on to your patience, I'm not through yet.
Let's turn it around and see what we get.

(THREE *prints the letters out in reverse from the last to the first and as the words emerge everyone shouts.*)

ALL TOGETHER. April Fool!

SUGGESTIONS

If this is actually presented in the classroom, on the first day of April, even the teacher could be surprised. You need only her approval and a signal to begin.

Of course you could use *Surprise* as a stage skit, setting the scene with school chairs and as many students as you wish. Certain changes would have to be made. To bring in the teacher might complicate things. Why not have someone announce that school has just begun, and although the class has assembled the teacher has not yet come in?

If it is given on a day other than the first of April it might be a good idea to have an April 1 date visible on a large calendar. Don't make that the only prop, however, or you'll give the idea away. Have an American flag, maybe a hanging map and of course you'll have to have something to serve as a blackboard.

Incidentally, the syncopation can be accented by having Two and Five, who remain seated, beat out the rhythm on their desks.

THE STORY OF JOHN WORTHINGTON SNEE

CHARACTERS

THE ANNOUNCER OF THE PROGRAM
THE PROFESSOR
JOHN WORTHINGTON SNEE, PIRATE
PIRATES, ANY NUMBER
GHOST OF SNEE'S MOTHER
JOHN WORTHINGTON SNEE, SHERIFF
BARTENDER
COWBOYS, ANY NUMBER
JOHN WORTHINGTON SNEE, FIREMAN
THE GIRL
FIREMEN, ANY NUMBER
JOHN WORTHINGTON SNEE, DETECTIVE
THE WITNESS
JOHN WORTHINGTON SNEE, SCHOOLBOY

ANNOUNCER. (*stepping out in front of the curtain*) Every once in awhile we come across an amazing personality whose story must be told. John Worthington Snee is such a one, and at this time I should like to present Professor Peak who has known Snee almost from the very beginning.

(*The* PROFESSOR *steps out in front of the curtain, acknowledges the introduction, and takes a position at the left side of the stage as the* ANNOUNCER *exits.*)

PROFESSOR.

So, you want to hear about Worthington Snee.
(*thoughtfully*) John Worthington Snee . . . well, let me see . . .
I hardly know where to begin on the lad.
Most remarkable student I ever had.
He came to me at the age of three
Knowing precisely what he would be
When he grew up . . . a pirate bold.
Fearless and daring and ruthless and cold.
(*The curtain opens on the pirate scene as the* PROFESSOR *continues*)
There he is now as he dreams he will be,
The fearsome, fabulous, cutthroat Snee.

SNEE. (*enters with fellow* PIRATES)

Come along, my hearties, he who digs best
Will first strike the iron of the buried chest.
Dig, my lads . . . dig about here (*he indicates the spot*)
And you'll unearth treasure, never you fear.
There'll be more gold to share and to spend
Than ever you'd find at the rainbow's end.
(*He walks to the footlights and speaks in confidence to the audience.*)
What they don't know is that I will see
That all the gold goes to Captain Snee . . . that's me.
(*somebody strikes something with a metallic ring*)
There! You have struck it! (*they pull out the chest*)
Now I'll do the rest.
I won't need you to open the chest.

You didn't think Snee would divide his find.
I'll pocket the gold and leave you behind.
Give all your guns and your knives to me,
And I'll tie you up to the nearest tree . . .
(*The* GHOST OF SNEE'S MOTHER *comes out and touches him on the shoulder and he reacts like a sheepish child.*)
Aw, gee, mom . . . I'm sorry. O.K. I'll play fair.
Come along fellows and take your share.

PROFESSOR.

Who's that? Well, you see, it's his mother's ghost.
He almost forgot that he was supposed
To be kind. He'd promised and crossed his heart.
This pirate business was wrong from the start. (*Curtain closes.*)
And so by the time young Snee was four
He'd changed his mind about pirate lore
And turned to the prairie. As Sheriff John Snee
He'd stand for the right, and when he told me
I said to myself, "Perhaps he aims
To track down fellows like Jesse James,
And Old Black Bart, and Billy the Kid."
And I guess in his dreams that's what he did.

(*Curtain opens on the western scene. Several* COWBOYS *sit around a table playing tiddlywinks or jacks or some other recognizable game of children and a* BARTENDER *stands behind a counter with his back to the audience.*)

FIRST COWBOY.

Have you seen the sheriff . . . the new man, Snee?

SECOND COWBOY.

Naw, but they say he's as tough as can be.
He's lookin' for outlaws . . . that's what they say.

FIRST COWBOY.

Well, I wish him luck . . . go on, it's your play.

(SNEE *enters with a gun in each hand.*)

SNEE.

I'm Sheriff John Snee, and I stand for the law.
I can lick any three men . . . I'm quick on the draw,
So throw down your guns, and we'll clean up this town.
(*Nobody pays any attention to him*)
Didn't you hear me? I said, throw them down.

FIRST COWBOY.

Gee whiz, Sheriff Snee, I don't have any gun,
And I don't think anyone in here has one.
Now if you like games, you're welcome to stay
But ya gotta keep quiet and let us play.

(*The* BARTENDER *turns around. He has on a ruffled apron and he sets out a sign:* TEA SERVED EVERY AFTERNOON AT FOUR. *Curtain.*)

PROFESSOR.

Well, the life of a sheriff had only one flaw
And after awhile even Worthington saw

That the Wild West he wanted to tame was dead.
The bad men were captured or filled with lead.
There wasn't a soul to outfight or outdraw;
It would grow pretty dull just upholding the law.
Worthington bowed to the hand of fate,
Deciding at five he was born too late.
He transferred his dreams of a ten gallon hat
To a fireman's red one, and that was that.
He could still be a hero, fearless and brave
And think of the hundreds of lives he would save.

(*Curtain opens on the fireman scene.* SNEE *and several others enter. They have come to rescue a* GIRL *from an upstairs window.*)

SNEE.

Come on, my lads, let's fight the fire.
The smoke is thick and the flames grow higher.

GIRL. Help! Help!

ONE OF THE FIREMEN.

Look up there in the window frame
A beautiful girl . . . she'll be caught in the flame.

SNEE.

Then I shall rescue her. (*to the girl*) Don't be afraid.
(*turning to the* FIREMEN) Get me a ladder . . . I'll climb to her aid. (FIREMEN *exit and* SNEE, *remembering something, speaks to the audience*) Climb did I say? I completely forgot.

Heights make me dizzy. Am I in a spot!
I can't climb ladders . . . when will I learn?
(*to the girl*) Sorry, young lady. You'll just have to burn.
(*Quick curtain.*)

PROFESSOR.

Yes, it was sad, for Worthington found
He couldn't fight fires and stay on the ground.
The dream of a fireman just wouldn't do.
He'd have to get busy and plan something new.
And at five-and-a-half he decided to be
A detective—J. W. Snee.
The joy of the city; the pride of the force,
This was his logical future, of course,
Because like the pirate he still could be bold
And like the sheriff the law he'd uphold
And as for the bravery of firemen . . . why pshaw.
A detective's as brave . . . at least it's a draw.
(*Curtain opens on detective scene.* SNEE *is questioning a witness.*)
There you see he's applying his skill
At getting the facts. Let's see if he will.

SNEE.

We just want the facts. Now what do you say?
Where were you the night of the third of May?

WITNESS.

Why I was in bed when I heard a scream.
I thought for awhile it was only a dream.

SNEE.

Don't bother with thought. We just want facts.
When did you first discover the tracks?

WITNESS.

Right after that. I just told you so.
I looked out the window and there below
Were these footprints . . . a lot of them too.
That's all I can tell you. Now are you through?

SNEE.

I guess that's all I need to know.
If you don't leave town, you can go. (*Witness exits.*)
I'll call the Captain now and see
If there's anything more he wants of me. (*phones*)
Hello, may I speak to the Captain please?
Snee reporting . . . *Snee* not *Sneeze.*
Hello, Captain, this is Snee.
What's that . . . the facts . . . well, let me see.
(*He starts looking for his notes.*)
I've got them, sir . . . I know they're here . . .
(*He searches through pockets and even under his hat and in his shoes.*) I took them down . . . oh dear . . . oh dear . . .
I can't have lost them . . . let me look. (*looks in book*)
No, no, they're not in that book.
Wait a minute, Captain . . . wait.
Oh dear, he's hung up. It's too late
I've been fired as of today.
The criminals will get away,

And just when I was close behind them.
I got the facts. I just can't find them. (*He sobs as the curtain closes.*)

PROFESSOR.

Well, there he was, a failure again.
Worthington turned in his badge and then
Resigned himself to meaningless dreams,
Having no heart for adventurous schemes.
And I lost track of the boy for awhile,
Remembering him now and again with a smile.
But then he reappeared out of the blue.
I wouldn't have known him . . . neither would you.
Grown to a ripe old age of six
He'd learned that dreaming and doing don't mix;
And doers are not just born . . . they're made.
You know what he did? He started first grade.

(*As the* PROFESSOR *exits,* SNEE, *the schoolboy, enters with a lunch box and books and runs across the stage in front of the curtain.*)

SNEE.

Hey wait for me . . . wait for me . . .

SUGGESTIONS

If the cast is too large for you, some people can play two or even three parts. The costumes will take little time to change. And if you wish to eliminate the announcer, the professor can take the lines, introducing himself. Incidentally, the professor has a great deal to memorize. He could read from a script as though it was a prepared speech. The character of Snee in each scene can be the same person or five different individuals.

The costumes are dictated by the roles. Boots and eye patches and ragged shirts for the pirates; a sheet for the ghost; jeans, cowboy hats for the cowboys and a ruffled apron for the bartender. Dig up firemen's hats if possible, and the detective might be dressed to suggest any classic sleuth or any current TV character. The professor might appear in cap and gown—an exaggeration, of course, but effective.

Props are also mentioned in the script. Knives and guns for the pirates and a treasure chest which incidentally can be covered with a blanket or canvas so that when it is "unearthed" it can actually be pulled out of hiding. A phone for the detective and naturally a notebook.

You needn't bother much with make-up except for a handlebar mustache on the bartender. The costumes and the lines will be enough to carry the idea.

The simplest solution to the burning building scene is to put it off-stage, and the girl need only be heard, not seen.

This skit lends itself well to Cub Scouts. Just substitute the following for the last four lines:

> Grown to the ripe old age of eight,
> A doer he is not the dreamer of late.
> Gone are his frivolous days and his doubts . . .
> You know what he did? He joined the Cub Scouts.

And in a final appearance Snee is a Cub Scout, giving the salute and perhaps the promise.

HERLOCK SHOLMES

CHARACTERS

HERLOCK SHOLMES, INSPECTOR OF YOTLAND SCARD

HENNESSEY, DENNESSEY, SMURTZ } THE THREE BEST MEN

LADY AGATHA, THE LADY OF THE HOUSE

LORD PETER, HER HUSBAND

GUESTS

SIR DAVID, THE ENTHUSIASTIC FELLOW WITH A BALLOON

SIR GARY, THE CHECKER PLAYER

SIR JOHN, THE SLEEPER

When the skit is announced, the auditorium is darkened for a minute. Then the footlights go on, but the curtain is closed. There is a potted flower plant at the left—petunias. HERLOCK SHOLMES *enters from the right.*

SHOLMES. (*to the audience*) Stay right where you are, ladies and gentlemen. No need to be alarmed. Let me introduce myself. Inspector Herlock Sholmes of Yotland Scard. At your service. A call just came in to our office from this place next to you. (*he indicates the stage*) It seems there's been . . . and keep this quiet now . . . we don't like these things to get about . . . it seems there's been a murder. I've sent for my three best men, Hennessey, Dennessey and Smurtz. And you may be sure the matter is in good hands. The motto of the Scard . . .

Look! Listen! and Leave No Stone Unturned! Ah here they are now. (HENNESSEY, DENNESSEY, *and* SMURTZ *have been moving up from the back of the auditorium and they now come onto the stage.*)

HENNESSEY. Hennessey . . .

DENNESSEY. Dennessey . . .

SMURTZ. And Smurtz . . .

HENNESSEY, DENNESSEY, SMURTZ. (*all together*) Reporting, sir.

SHOLMES. Hennessey, you have the notes on the case?

HENNESSEY. Right here, sir. (*He takes the notes from his pocket and lets fall a long paper that drops section by section until it touches the floor.*)

SHOLMES. You are to watch all suspicious characters, find the guilty person, and then send for me. (*turns to* DENNESSEY) Dennessey?

DENNESSEY. Yes, sir?

SHOLMES. Now you are to look for clues. Nothing must be overlooked.

DENNESSEY. I won't miss a thing, sir.

SHOLMES. (*moves on to* SMURTZ) And Smurtz?

SMURTZ. Yes, sir?

SHOLMES. You have the most important job of all. Go to the house. Say you are making a fire inspection and then . . . and then . . . let me see, I was sure there was something important for you to do.

SMURTZ. Could it be to find the body, sir?

SHOLMES. Oh, yes, to be sure . . . the body. You Smurtz are to find the body. And one thing more . . . when you get inside draw the curtains here at the French window so that I, Herlock Sholmes, can watch unobserved. Remember the motto . . .

HENNESSEY. Look!

DENNESSEY. Listen!

SMURTZ. And Leave No Stone Unturned. (*The three exit and* HERLOCK SHOLMES *turns to the audience.*) No one will notice me here behind the petunias. (*He hides as the curtain opens.*)

(*On the stage* SIR DAVID *is walking about listlessly waving a balloon and blowing out one of those party whistles. At a table in the center of the stage,* SIR GARY *and* SIR JOHN *sit with a checker board between them.* SIR JOHN *is asleep and* SIR GARY *continues the game by himself, playing both sides.* DENNESSEY *comes in from the right with his magnifying glass and knapsack. He inspects everything minutely and every now and then he tucks something into his kit. He ends up back at the right side of the stage just as* LADY AGATHA *enters from the left followed closely by* HENNESSEY.)

AGATHA. (*to* SIR DAVID) Sir David, are you enjoying yourself?

SIR DAVID. Oh, yes. I'm having a delightful time . . . a delightful time. (*He speaks in a monotone and waves his balloon. There is no expression on his face.*)

AGATHA. Have you seen Lord Peter? I've looked everywhere for him.

SIR DAVID. I'm sure he hasn't been in here, Lady Agatha. I've been here all evening . . . just having a delightful time.

AGATHA. He couldn't possibly have escaped your eagle eye, Sir David. I do hope he hasn't overindulged in the lemonade. He really must be watched carefully at a party. (*She pauses to watch the checker game.*) I don't suppose you gentlemen have seen him? (JOHN *snores and* GARY *keeps right on with his game.*) No, I guess you haven't. (*She walks about a little more with* HENNESSEY *at her heels. She looks under chairs and other unlikely places for* LORD PETER. SMURTZ *enters from the right in fireman's hat and long coat.*)

SMURTZ. (*shouting*) Fire inspection. Stay just as you are, folks. Stay just as you are. (*Exits.*)

AGATHA. Odd time for fire inspection. And you know, I have the strangest feeling that I'm being followed. (*She doesn't realize that* HENNESSEY *is right behind her.*)

DENNESSEY. (*concentrating on his magnifying glass and practically on his hands and knees, comes upon Hennessey's shoes*) Oh, it's you, old chap. We'll have to close this case soon. I have my knapsack quite full of clues . . . no room for more.

HENNESSEY. Then we'll just bag the old girl now. Must be her, you know. She seems to be the only one alive. (*He takes* LADY AGATHA *by the arm.*) Come along. You can't get by with crime while Yotland Scard is on the job. Call the Inspector, Dennessey. Let's get on with the thing. (DENNESSEY *exits to join* SHOLMES.)

AGATHA. Get on with the thing. What is the meaning of this, sir? Crime, you say? Is it a crime these days to look for one's husband. It's his party, you know. He really ought to be here.

SHOLMES. (*to* DENNESSEY) We'll just go in here through the window . . . (*They join the group, pantomiming the opening of the French windows and stepping over the sill.*) What seems to be the trouble? Who are you, madam?

AGATHA. I might ask you the same, sir. I am Lady Agatha Dalrimple. I am simply giving a party for my husband. It's his birthday. Only I can't seem to find him. This man suddenly seized me. Who are *you?*

SHOLMES. You mean you don't know? I, madam, am Inspector Herlock Sholmes of Yotland Scard. I understand that there's been a murder here.

AGATHA. Murder . . . murder! There's been no murder here.

SHOLMES. Lady Agatha, did you or did you not call my office at precisely seven-fifty-nine-and-a-half and report a murder on your estate?

AGATHA. Most certainly not.

SHOLMES. How about your guests?

AGATHA. (*she looks around at* SIR DAVID *and* SIR GARY *and* SIR JOHN) That hardly seems possible, but we'll ask them. Sir David . . .

SIR DAVID. Delightful time . . . simply delightful . . .

AGATHA. Did you call Yotland Scard to report a murder?

SIR DAVID. Oh, indeed not, Lady Agatha. Why would I? When I'm having such a delightful time.

AGATHA. Sir Gary, did you report a murder at eight o'clock?

SHOLMES. Seven-fifty-nine-and-a-half.

SIR GARY. (*who is hard of hearing*) Eh?

AGATHA. Murder, Sir Gary, murder. Did you call Yotland Scard?

SIR GARY. (*cupping his ear*) Hard? Yes this fellow is hard to beat, but the game will be over in a minute now. I've got him in a corner.

AGATHA. You see. As for Sir John . . . he's been asleep since six-thirty.

SHOLMES. Then we shall approach this from another angle. Hennessey?

HENNESSEY. Reporting, sir.

SHOLMES. Did you take the message which reached us at seven-fifty-nine-and-a-half this evening?

HENNESSEY. I got it from Dennessey, sir.

SHOLMES. Dennessey?

DENNESSEY. Reporting, sir.

SHOLMES. Did you take the message which reached us at seven-fifty-nine-and-a-half this evening?

DENNESSEY. I got it from Smurtz, sir.

SHOLMES. (*calling out*) Smurtz!

(SMURTZ *enters excitedly from the left.*)

SMURTZ. Eureka! I found it, sir . . . the body!

AGATHA. I think I'm going to faint.

SMURTZ. (*to* HENNESSEY) You'll have to lend a hand out here.

(*They exit.* DENNESSEY *rushes to* LADY AGATHA'*s aid, fanning her and patting her hand.* SMURTZ *and* HENNESSEY *enter again, half carrying, half dragging* LORD PETER *onto the stage.*)

AGATHA. That's not a body, that's Lord Peter. Where in the world have you been? How thoughtless to play dead at your own party. (*she goes over and sniffs at him*) Just as I thought. Steeped in lemonade again. Peter, what have you to say? Speak to me.

LORD PETER. (*gruffly*) Hello.

SHOLMES. Why don't you ask *him?*

AGATHA. Lord Peter, did you make a call to Yotland Scard this evening?

LORD PETER. I did.

SHOLMES. And what did you say?

LORD PETER. I told them to give Herlock Sholmes a message from me.

SHOLMES. The message, sir, the message? What was it?

LORD PETER. I'd rather not say . . . in front of Lady Agatha.

AGATHA. Oh for heaven's sake, Lord Peter. Let's get this straightened out.

LORD PETER. Promise you won't be angry?

AGATHA. Why should I be angry?

SHOLMES. What was the message?

LORD PETER. (*sheepishly*) Come over at once. The party is dead.

SHOLMES. The party is *dead!*

HENNESSEY, DENNESSEY, SMURTZ. The party is *dead?*

LORD PETER. (*indicates the inactivity around them*) Well, isn't it? I'm sorry, Aggie, but it's true. Jolly well the deadest party I've ever attended. (*Very quick curtain.*)

> (HERLOCK SHOLMES *and his men come out in front of the closed curtain.*)

SHOLMES. Well that's another case closed . . . and true to the tradition of Yotland Scard.

> (*He exits.* HENNESSEY *plays a pair of binoculars around the auditorium as he follows* SHOLMES. DENNESSEY *cups first one ear and then the other and exits through the center opening of the curtain.*

SMURTZ *just stands looking about him, and then he exits. There is a moment of quiet until* SMURTZ *returns weighted down with a large stone. He sets it down, then deliberately turns it over. On the back is printed:* THE STONE IS TURNED.)

SUGGESTIONS

Success here depends on exaggeration to the point of being ridiculous. The detective is of another time and place and the lines are stilted and old-fashioned. By delivering them with great seriousness you will achieve humor. Hennessey, Dennessey, and Smurtz will snap to attention at the voice of their inspector, and Sholmes will be the last word in formality and dignity in dealing with Lady Agatha.

The costumes should be equally overdone in the spirit of the thing. If you can't get a Sherlock Holmes cap, make one, perhaps by fitting one cap over another so that you have a double bill, back and front. Of course the sleuth should have a pipe, and the player might even try an English accent just for the fun of it.

Why not dress Hennessey, Dennessey, and Smurtz in identical outfits? After all, their speeches are often repetitive. Give Lady Agatha sweeping skirts, and provide a monocle for at least one of the party guests.

The props are more important than the costuming. The magnifying glass (make it a big one), the knapsack, the long, long list of notes. And why not squeaky shoes for Hennessey? A toy mouse in the player's hand will do the trick. Don't forget the checker board, the balloon, and the party toy for Sir David, and finally the stone that's turned. If you think the audience won't be able to see the printing on it, put up a little placard. Always be sure the point is clear.

Incidentally, the potted plant which is to hide Sholmes doesn't have to be petunias. The lines can always be changed to accommodate the prop man.

NESTER THE JESTER

CHARACTERS

NESTER, THE JESTER

BOYS, ONE, TWO, AND THREE

THE KING

THE QUEEN

THE PRINCESS

SIR ECHO

SIR ECHO'S FRIEND

THE GREEN KNIGHT

As the sketch opens, something resembling a huge book is pushed out onto the stage in front of the closed curtain by the THREE BOYS. *The title,* KNIGHTS OF THE SQUARE TABLE, *is clearly printed on the book's cover.*

BOY ONE. Where did you get this thing anyhow?

BOY TWO. Down at my dad's book store. He had it in his window . . . for advertising.

BOY THREE. Well, I'm glad I don't have to read a book as big as this. It would take me a year.

BOY ONE. I don't think it has any pages in it. Anyway it ought to be good for something. We can just leave it here while we think.

(The BOYS *turn to exit when the book rips open, and the* JESTER *tumbles out. He gets up, dusts himself off, and then he sees the* BOYS.)

JESTER. Wait. Don't go away. Can you tell me where I am?

BOY ONE. On the stage of course. That's a silly question.

BOY TWO. That's not what he means. Didn't you see where he came from? I'll tell you where you are. You're in America.

JESTER. America? Never heard of it. What year is it? (*his face lights up in anticipation*)

BOY THREE. 19–, of course. (*current date*), 19–. At least that's what I put on my spelling paper.

JESTER. Hurrah! I made it. I did. I did. Do you know who *I* am?

BOY ONE. You look like a clown to me.

JESTER. Well, that's close . . . not a clown, but something like one. Let me introduce myself. I'm Nester the Jester.

BOY TWO. Oh, I know about jesters. They were kept around by the kings to amuse the court.

JESTER. Well, here's one that got away. At least for a little while.

VOICE OF THE KING OFFSTAGE. Where is that fool jester, Nester? Where is he, I say.

JESTER. Oh, oh. They've discovered that I've gone. Sh! Let's be quiet. Maybe they'll stop looking for me. (*They listen.*)

VOICE OF THE KING. (*growing fainter*) Nester! Nester! Where are you . . . .

BOY TWO. Why don't you want them to know where you are?

JESTER. Because we have a problem and there doesn't seem to be any solution to it in there. (*He points to the book.*) I thought maybe if I advanced a century or two, I could get help.

BOY THREE. What's the problem?

JESTER. Have you ever heard of Sir Echo?

BOY ONE. Sure. We all have. (*They start to sing* "Little Sir Echo.")

JESTER. No. No. That's not the one. I mean Sir Echo of the Square Table.

BOY ONE. Never heard of *him.*

JESTER. You have now. Help me push this thing out of the way. (*They all push the book to the far left and the*

JESTER *continues.*) If you concentrate maybe you can see what's going on back there. Close your eyes and think *hard.*

(*As they follow his instruction the curtain opens. The* KING *is pacing the floor. The* QUEEN *and the* PRINCESS *are seated at the right. The* PRINCESS *is sobbing.*)

KING. Where can he be? That Nester jester is supposed to make me laugh. Especially when I don't feel like laughing. And I never felt less like laughing than I do now.

JESTER. (*to the* BOYS) That's my boss, the King. I don't wonder he misses me. He's very dull.

QUEEN. I don't know why you're upset about that foolish jester. Laughter isn't going to do anything to help Sir Echo.

JESTER. That's the Queen. She should talk. She isn't much help either. Not with this kind of problem. (*The* PRINCESS *sobs noisily.*)

QUEEN. The Princess is crying her eyes out. There, there, dear. I guess you'll just have to put Sir Echo out of your thoughts. (*The* PRINCESS *sobs louder.*)

JESTER. Now you're beginning to get the problem. You see the Princess is very fond of Sir Echo and . . .

BOY TWO. What's wrong with that?

JESTER. You'll see. Here comes Sir Echo now. And that's his best friend with him.

(*Enter* SIR ECHO *and* FRIEND)

FRIEND. You don't look like much of a knight without any armor.

ECHO. You know I can't even stand up with that hardware on. It's pretty discouraging.

FRIEND. You're right there. But let's try again. (*He hands* ECHO *a sword.*) Hold this while I find your helmet.

ECHO. (*as he takes the sword in his right hand he becomes overbalanced by it and topples to the floor*) It's just no use. I can't even hold it . . . let alone wield it.

FRIEND. (*helping him to his feet and taking the sword back*) Don't give up. Try a few more knee bends. (*The two of them do a few exercises.*)

JESTER. Poor little Echo. He's got about as much strength as . . . well an echo. You see he can't win the hand of the Princess until he defeats the Green Knight in hand-to-hand combat. There, that's the problem.

BOY THREE. I'll say.

JESTER. How can he fight any kind of a knight, blue, green or white, when he hasn't the might to lift the sword. He's brave enough, but he hasn't the strength. I wish I could help him. I've tried everything. (ECHO *attempts to lift the sword again and fails.*) Here comes the guy he has to defeat. Now you'll see something else. (*The* GREEN KNIGHT *enters.*)

GREEN KNIGHT. Stand aside! (SIR ECHO *doesn't hear the command because he is absorbed in his practice, and the* GREEN KNIGHT *picks him up and sets him aside and exits.*)

ECHO. (*crying on his* FRIEND*'s shoulder*) It's just no use, I tell you.

BOY TWO. (*to* NESTER) Wait a minute. I think you came to the right place. I've got an idea. (*He whispers to the other* BOYS.)

BOY THREE. It's worth a try. (*He exits.*)

JESTER. I sure do hope you can help. I just can't stand to see Echo so unhappy. (*He forgets that he is in a different time and place than* ECHO *and calls out to him.*) Sir Echo! Oh Sir Echo!

ECHO. (*squints as though through a screen and from a long distance*) Nester? Is that you? Where are you?

JESTER. Here I am . . . out here. I don't think you can see me.

ECHO. Well, no matter. Don't you know the King's been looking all over for you. You'd better come back. (*He moves toward* NESTER *as though through some kind of barrier.*) Now I can see you.

(*He takes the* JESTER*'s arm.* BOY THREE *enters again with a brown paper sack and as* ECHO *pulls the* JESTER *toward him* BOY THREE *thrusts the sack in the* JESTER*'s hands.*)

BOY THREE. Here . . . here's a bit of modern magic. Give it to your friend. And come back and see us again sometime. (*The* BOYS *exit.*)

JESTER. (*calling back as he moves to the center of the stage*) Thanks. Thanks. I will if I can ever get away again. (*Then he turns to* ECHO.) Never mind about the King. I've been out there in some place called America . . .

ECHO. Where?

JESTER. You wouldn't understand. Anyhow I've brought back a magic remedy.

ECHO. (*turns away*) Not a potion, I hope. The last one I tried was horrible . . . with spiders and toads and hummingbird's feathers. Besides it was a nauseating green. And green isn't my favorite color right now.

JESTER. I don't know what color it is. Just take it. If there are any directions, follow them. I'll see you at the tournament.

(*Curtain closes and opens again almost at once. There is a blare of trumpets. The* PRINCESS *enters with the* QUEEN *and is still crying. The* KING *follows them onto the stage as the* JESTER *enters from the opposite side.*)

KING. (*seeing* NESTER) There you are. Don't you know I've been scouring the countryside for you?

JESTER. Sorry m'lord, and all the court, but I've found something of great import. You'll see, you'll see when they start the sport. Attend! Attend!

KING. Well, don't go away again. Echo has been in terrible shape, and the Princess makes me nervous.

(*The* KING *claps his hands and the* GREEN KNIGHT *and* SIR ECHO *enter.* SIR ECHO *is wearing his armor and sword and he also carries the paper sack which he gives to* NESTER *for safekeeping.*)

QUEEN. Sir Echo is wearing his armor!

KING. And his sword!

(*The* PRINCESS *stops crying long enough to look. The trumpet blares again and the fight begins.* ECHO *is victorious and the* GREEN KNIGHT *is carried off. The* PRINCESS *throws her handkerchief to* ECHO *and then exits with the* QUEEN.)

KING. (*to* ECHO) Confidentially, Echo, how did you manage this? Yesterday you didn't have the strength to swat a fly.

ECHO. It was the magic of Nester, your majesty . . .

KING. (*turns to* NESTER) O.K., Nester. What's your magic?

JESTER. Mum's the word, m'lord. Would you want to spoil the charm?

KING. Heaven forbid. I don't think I could stand another seige of the Princess' crying. I'm willing to let well enough alone. But don't you leave me again.

(KING *and* ECHO *exit and* NESTER *who lags behind speaks to the audience.*)

JESTER. Thanks, you fellows out there. (*he pulls a package of whatever body-building cereal is popular out of the brown sack*) When Echo runs out I'll get back to you somehow. Keep your books open.

(*There is a quick curtain as the* JESTER *runs after the* KING.)

SUGGESTIONS

The book from which the jester emerges might be made from a large carton. Cut away the three sides leaving two for the covers and one for the binding. If the binding section is too wide, it can be cut and overlapped to suit your wishes. Any lightweight paper, lined a bit to resemble page edges, can be fitted across the space from one cover to the other and taped in place. It is through this paper that the jester will tumble. Be sure that the title, *Knights of the Square Table,* is printed in big enough letters to be seen by the audience.

Costumes will be interesting to put together. Find some pictures of court jesters to get ideas for Nester. Slippers and a floppy pointed hat, both with bells attached, colored tights and some kind of a tunic. And how about clown style make-up?

Give the king a purple cape over tights and tunic and of course a crown.

Queen and princess need only long skirts and long-sleeved blouses. A crown on the queen will identify her, and the princess might have one of those cone-shaped headpieces with a scarf flowing from the tip of it.

Tunics and tights for the Green Knight and Echo, and then for the fight scene provide shields of cardboard covered with aluminum foil. Paper sacks sprayed with silver paint with the proper facial cutouts will work very well as helmets, and if you want more armor make and spray cardboard breastplates as well.

GWENDOLYN GLORIA GERTRUDE McFEE

CHARACTERS

MRS. MC FEE, GWENDOLYN'S MOTHER
GWENDOLYN, PRINCESS
THE CLERK
GWENDOLYN, OPERA STAR
GWENDOLYN, NURSE
PATIENT I, THE SOCIALITE
PATIENT II, THE DOCTOR'S WIFE
PATIENT III, THE CHILD
THE CHILD'S MOTHER
THE TEACHER
GWENDOLYN, POLITICIAN
THE ATTENDANT
GWENDOLYN, MOTHER
THE CHILDREN, KATE, NORA, HELEN, SHIRLEY, MARY, SUE

The skit opens with a closed curtain. MRS. MC FEE *steps out from the right and remains at the side of the stage.*

MRS. MC FEE.

I've been asked for the story of Gertrude McFee . . .
Gwendolyn Gloria Gertrude . . . you see
I am her mother and played a great part
In my daughter's development right from the start.
Gwendolyn Gloria at the age of three
Was very sure what she would be
When she grew up . . . a princess fair,
With dancing feet and golden hair. (*Curtain opens.*

There is a desk at the left with a clerk seated behind it.)

There . . . (MRS. MC FEE *indicates the* PRINCESS *who has entered and moves gracefully about.*) that is how she expected to look . . .

Right from the pages of her storybook.

PRINCESS. (*pauses in her movement and speaks to the audience*)

It's all very well to have beauty galore,
But I need a kingdom to rule . . . and what's more
I need a prince . . . (*she goes to the desk*) A handsome prince charming.

CLERK.

The shortage of princes is most alarming
And as for kingdoms . . . there's nothing to spare,
Not even for rulers with golden hair.
I'm sorry, my dear, but we cannot deny
The demand just simply exceeds the supply.

(*Curtain closes.*)

MRS. MC FEE.

So she gave up her crown, put those dreams in a drawer
And when Gwendolyn Gloria Gertrude was four
She turned to the stage. She'd be a great star
Of the opera, with fame flung afar.
She fancied herself as she would appear
At the Met, with voice true and clear.

(GWENDOLYN *as opera star enters from the left in front of the closed curtain. She sings very badly, stops, starts again, and as the audience boos, she breaks into sobs.*)

OPERA STAR.

All right then, I'll stop. There is no need to boo,
But how would you feel if this had been you? (*She exits left.*)

MRS. MC FEE.

Well, you saw what occurred . . . an unfortunate thing.
She was lovely to look at; she just couldn't sing.
But Gloria Gertrude at five, undaunted,
Decided that what she really wanted
Was to serve the world, and it might hail
A second Florence Nightingale.

(*Curtain opens on the doctor's office. There is a desk at the left and two chairs at the center back where* PATIENT I *and* II *are seated.* GWENDOLYN, *as nurse, enters from the left.*)

NURSE.

Good morning ladies. I'm nurse McFee.
The doctor's busy, but I am free
To give advice and to treat your ills,
Look at your throats and give you pills.

PATIENT I.

Well, if I'm to pay the doctor's fee,
It's the doctor I intend to see

Not the nurse. I'll simply wait,
Even though it's getting late.

PATIENT II.
And I'm the doctor's wife, my dear.
I'm going shopping, and I'm here
For money, and I don't think you
Could help me if you wanted to.

(PATIENT III, *the* CHILD, *is pulled into the office by her* MOTHER *who is out of breath.*)

MOTHER.
Excuse me, please . . . I tried to call . . .
My little girl has had a fall.
She cut her knee. It's bleeding too.
I'm sure you'll tell me what to do.

NURSE.
Of course I will. Bring her to me.
We'll fix her up . . . now, let me see. (*She takes off the handkerchief which is wrapped around the girl's leg and takes one look.*) Oh, it *is* bleeding . . . oh . . . I say . . . (*faints*)

CHILD. Mama! She fainted dead away. (*Quick curtain.*)

MRS. MC FEE.
That's right. Poor Gwendolyn Gertrude found
When she saw blood her head spun round.
She had no choice but to concur.
To be a nurse was not for her.

And now the girl was quite downhearted
I felt it was high time she started
To school, and with some trepidation
She began her education.
And now I think it only fair
Her teacher take the story there. (*The* TEACHER *enters left.*)

TEACHER. (*taking a position at the left of the closed curtain directly opposite* MRS. MC FEE)
Good evening, I'm Ms. Lois Heath
Educated to the teeth,
B.A., M.A., and Ph.D.
Wise she was to come to me
For learning, and I do remember
Gertrude well. It was September
When she came to join my class.
In beauty, brain, none could surpass.
And at the early age of six
She'd changed her field to politics.
She didn't think she'd have to sing.
There'd be no blood or anything
To make her ill. Might be all right
She'd only need a cause to fight
For and a voice just good and loud
With which to stir an eager crowd. (*enter* GWENDOLYN, *politician*)
Here she comes . . . let's listen in.
(GWENDOLYN *turns toward the* TEACHER *as though for approval*)
Go on, my dear, go on, begin . . .

POLITICIAN.

Ladies of this great wide land
I'm here to tell you where I stand
Upon the issue. Come unite
And then demand the selfsame right
To vote that men have had down through
The years. *We want it too.*

ATTENDANT. (*enters from the wings*)

I'm sorry, madam, it would seem
Your issue's slightly off the beam.
Unite we did and fought aplenty,
But that was back in nineteen-twenty.

POLITICIAN.

Oh, dear me, if this is true,
Politically, I fear I'm through. (*Exits quickly.*)

(*The* TEACHER *watches her leave and then speaks to the audience.*)

TEACHER.

Poor Gloria Gertrude . . . born too late
For the cause she wanted to debate.
I wonder if she didn't know
The vote was granted long ago?
That women now, across the nation,
Are speaking out for liberation?
Well, one career pursued the other.
At last she said she'd be a mother,

With quite a few children, six maybe seven,
And each one an angel right out of heaven.
She'd never be cross, never be stern.
All of her darlings would very soon learn
Their mother was different . . . would not get upset.

MRS. MC FEE. And that was the craziest dream she had yet. (*Curtain opens.*)

TEACHER. (*indicating the entrance of* GWENDOLYN *as mother with the* CHILDREN.)
There she comes now, and it can't be denied
Mama McFee is fit to be tied.

KATE. Mama, take me to the zoo.

NORA. The zoo. The zoo. Take me too.

(KATE *and* NORA *pull at their mother's coat.*)

MOTHER.
Not today, and please don't cry
If you are good, I'll really try . . .
Stop pulling at me. Mary,
You are much too big to carry.

HELEN.
Mama, make Sue leave me be
I haven't got her dolly . . . see (*she holds out her hands*)

MOTHER.

Kate, stop playing in the dirt
Helen, have you torn your skirt? (SHIRLEY *runs in from the left.*)

SHIRLEY.

Mama, mama, come and look
Tommy's fallen in the brook. (*They all start to shout.*)

MOTHER.

Children, will you stop your shouting
We'll never take another outing.
I, for one, admit defeat.
We're going home. I'm simply beat. (*Curtain closes as they exit.*)

TEACHER.

It was all very sad, for Gertrude found out
There were times she wanted to scream and to shout.
Her patience grew thin, her nerves were unsteady.
For motherhood, Gertrude just wasn't ready.
Well, there she was, a failure again.
Gwendolyn gave up her children and then
I lost track of the girl for awhile
Remembering her now and again with a smile
Until she appeared one day out of the blue.
I didn't know her, and neither would you.
Grown to the ripe old age of nine
She told me that everything turned out fine.
Her smile was enchanting; her manner was mild.
You know, she'd decided to be . . . just a child.

(*The curtain opens slightly and the smallest of the children in the mother sketch comes out as the* TEACHER *exits.*)

CHILD. (*speaking rapidly in a high-pitched monotone*) And with all the problems grownups have these days that's not bad. (*She exits back through the curtain again.*)

SUGGESTIONS

Except for costuming and carry-on props, very little is needed for this skit—perhaps a desk or table and two or three chairs for the princess scene and the doctor's office. The politician should bring on a soap box from which to speak, and you might have an "Employment Service" sign for the princess bit.

Have fun with the costumes. The mother might wear simply what mothers are wearing, and the teacher might be in a suit and have a hat on, as though she had just arrived to speak her piece. Incidentally, it might add humor if the teacher is patterned after a favorite in the school, someone the audience knows, and her real name could be listed in the cast of characters. The children who are called by name in the script can use their own names too, if it is easier.

Do as much as you wish with costumes. The princess could wear something long and silky, with a crown on her head of course. The opera star should be a comic character. Give her long strings of pearls over a much too large black formal. Have someone planted in the audience to boo her, and be sure she has a large handkerchief to produce when her tears fall.

For the nurse, try to get a white uniform or at least a white dress and shoes. You can always make a nurse's cap out of paper. The adult patient, the doctor's wife, and the mother with all the children can wear street clothes suitable to whatever age you have selected for them. The politician will do well in tailored clothes, possibly a suit, and with sensible shoes.

This sketch would adapt well to Girl Scouts. Just change the last four lines:

Nothing could match the glow on her face
When she told me she'd finally found her place
And was ever so glad for the way things turned out..
You know what she was? A full-fledged Girl Scout.

Or how about Camp Fire Girls? Then you might have as the last four lines:

Nothing could match the glow on her face
When she told me she'd finally found her place
And was no longer caught in an aimless whirl.
You know what she was? A Camp Fire Girl.

Gwendolyn, as Scout or Camp Fire Girl, should enter quickly just as the teacher comes to the last phrase.

There are a lot of characters here, and you might want to double up. Just be sure to allow for any costume change. The opera star would hardly have time to change to the nurse's uniform.

HOW DID WE MANAGE BEFORE THE POSTMAN CAME?

CHARACTERS

THE ANNOUNCER
FATHER TIME
CAVEMAN
HERODOTUS
DIRTY DAN, WANTED
THE POSTMASTER
LUKE, JED, SAM—MEN OF THE OLD WEST
THE "LONELY HEARTS" GAL
BOB, BILL—JUST BOYS

The curtain is closed as the ANNOUNCER *steps in front of it.*

ANNOUNCER. Everybody knows that today when you have something to tell a person who lives a good distance away you write a letter. Oh, of course you could phone, but if you're long-winded it could be pretty expensive. So you get paper and pencil or pen, write what you wish, put it in an envelope, address it, stamp it, and mail it. You take this system for granted. But it took a long time to make this kind of communication possible. I introduce now the fellow who can tell us how it all began, because he was there. (*As* FATHER TIME *enters from the right also in front of the closed curtain, the* ANNOUNCER *exits.*)

FATHER TIME. I am Father Time. Long, long ago, about 2500 B.C. when I was . . . well, not as old as I am now

. . . man was a simple creature. He wanted only food and warmth and safety. At first he was interested only in himself, but he soon found that he could profit by helping his fellow. And so when Mr. Caveman spotted a herd of animals, which meant food, he wanted to tell his friend about it. Remember he couldn't write a letter. In fact he couldn't write at all, and even his speech was a series of grunts. Let's watch what he did.

(*The curtain opens. There is a huge rock at center stage, and the* CAVEMAN *enters, draws a crude sketch on its surface, a sketch of a great horned animal, with an arrow pointing in the direction it could be found. Then the* CAVEMAN *exits.*)

FATHER TIME. You see he has left his message. It will be quite plain to the friend when he comes this way. But, as I said, that was long ago. (*Curtain closes.*)

(HERODOTUS *hurries on from the left.*)

HERODOTUS. Aren't you about ready for me? I can't wait all day. I'm a busy man.

FATHER TIME. (*waves him to silence*) Just a minute. (*speaks to the audience again*) In the time that followed, man settled on some kind of language and some kind of written symbols, and by 560 B.C. in one spot in the world at least there existed a kind of postal service. Fortunately (*he glances at the impatient* HERODOTUS), or maybe unfortunately, there was a historian of that day to tell us about it.

HERODOTUS. I am Herodotus, the Greek historian . . .

FATHER TIME. Frankly he's a very dull fellow.

HERODOTUS. It is I who wrote of the postal service of King Cyrus of Persia. "Nothing mortal travels as fast as these Persian messengers. Neither snow nor rain nor heat nor gloom of night stays these couriers from their swift completion of their appointed rounds."

FATHER TIME. (*to audience*) Ever heard that before?

HERODOTUS. Of course they have. Twenty-four hundred years later my words were placed across the front of a great postal building in New York City . . . the motto of mail carriers of the twentieth century.

FATHER TIME. O.K. You've had your time. That's enough . . . enough of the olden days. (*He waves* HERODOTUS *off.*) Let's skip over the centuries. There are roads now, and paper and ink and printing. We come to a colorful period in the development of western America—the era of the stagecoach.

(*The curtain opens on the general store of Red Clay Gulch. There is a kind of counter and a sign which says* POSTMASTER ON DUTY HERE. DIRTY DAN *slouches in a chair off to one side;* JED *and* SAM *lean against the counter; the* POSTMASTER *busies himself with the mail.* LUKE *enters excitedly. He scratches his shoulders and chest as though plagued with fleas.*)

LUKE. Stage in yet?

POSTMASTER. Nope.

(LUKE *exits, still scratching.*)

JED. Wonder what old Luke's waitin' for. Cain't be expectin' any letters. He don't write none.

SAM. He cain't . . . cain't write. (*They all laugh.*)

LUKE. (*entering again*) I heard that. Say, ain't that stage overdue?

POSTMASTER. (*checks his watch*) About four hours. Ought to be along soon. Less they had trouble.

JED. What ya waitin' for, Luke?

LUKE. None of your business.

JED. I'll bet you're waitin' for the passenger. The word is there's a gal on the stage.

LUKE. Well, I ain't waitin' for no gal. (*Exits.*)

JED. How about you, Sam? You waitin' for the stage?

SAM. I reckon everybody waits . . . maybe even him. (*He nods to* DAN.)

POSTMASTER. He ain't been in town long. How about it, stranger? You interested in the stage? (DAN *doesn't answer.*)

JED. Come on . . . you been asked a question.

DAN. No law says I have to answer.

POSTMASTER. (*whispers*) Aw, let him alone. He's a tough one. Seen him over at Joe's last night, and the lead was flyin'.

JED. (*turns to* SAM) What's your interest, Sam? You expectin' a letter?

POSTMASTER. Maybe more'n a letter. Didn't you know he was corresponding with a gal outa Julesburg?

JED. How about that. Is she a good looker, Sam?

POSTMASTER. He don't know yet . . . never seen her. He got her name out of a lonely heart's column. He oughta get the picture of her today.

SAM. You mind your own business. And you better stop readin' my mail.

POSTMASTER. It's my legal right, Sam. Got to watch for trouble. There's a war goin' on, ya know.

JED. Don't get touchy, Sam. He don't mean no harm.

LUKE. (*entering from the right*) That stage runs later every week.

JED. Last week they didn't get here at all.

POSTMASTER. (*looking off-stage to the right*) Here she comes, boys!

(*There is shouting outside and the sound of horses and men. A mail bag is tossed onto the stage and the* POSTMASTER *starts to open it.*)

JED. There sure was a gal aboard. Here she comes. (*The* GIRL *enters.*) Lookin' for somebody, lady?

GIRL. Well, now, I'm Elvira Miggs. (SAM*'s jaw drops and he edges toward the door.*) Is there someone here named Sam?

(*The* POSTMASTER *nods toward* SAM, *and* ELVIRA *takes off after him.*)

GIRL. Wait . . . my little prairie dog . . . wait . . . wait . . .

(SAM *exits with* ELVIRA *on his heels. The* POSTMASTER *gets a circular out of the mail bag and posts it as* DAN *sneaks out.* ELVIRA *comes back onto the stage pulling* SAM *with her.*)

GIRL. I just figured I'd come in the flesh instead of sendin' my picture. No use to waste any more time.

POSTMASTER. (*who has pulled a package out of the bag*) Hey, Luke. This what you're waitin' for?

LUKE. Give it here.

POSTMASTER. Good-sized box, Luke. (*He shakes it, but he holds it out of reach.*) What's in it?

LUKE. None of your business. Give it here.

POSTMASTER. Might be unlawful merchandise . . . better be inspected . . .

LUKE. You give that here now . . . you got no right.

(POSTMASTER *opens the package and takes out a paper from the inside.*)

POSTMASTER. (*reading*) "Stop scratching. Change to summer weight."

(*As* LUKE *continues to protest and tries to grab the box, the* POSTMASTER *holds up long underwear. Everyone laughs as the curtain closes.*)

FATHER TIME. (*who has been watching all this time*) Those were interesting days all right. But they are gone too. Now we are in a time when even a child can use the mails . . . write letters and receive . . . well, you'll see.

(*Curtain opens.* BOB *and* BILL, *two contemporary boys are seated at the table. There are stacks of cereal boxes all around them and on the table as well.*)

BOB. We'd better check off the list once again, Bill.

BILL. O.K. Twenty boxtops from Frazzled Wheat . . . two space helmets.

BOB. Check.

BILL. Ten front panels from Toastie Posties . . . two cosmic ray guns.

BOB. Check.

BILL. Seven round lids from Ogilby's Oats . . . two bags of plastic moon rocks.

BOB. Check.

BILL. Seventeen labels from Bubbly Barley . . . one map of the solar system and two galactic code books.

BOB. Check. Well, I guess that's it. Have you got your money?

BILL. Yeah. You got yours?

BOB. I'm going to ask mom now. Come on.

BILL. What will we do with all this stuff. (*indicates boxes*)

BOB. Oh, just leave it. Mom will want me to take it to the kitchen later, I suppose.

BILL. Who's gonna eat it all anyhow?

BOB. Dad, of course. I hate the junk.

(*They exit with their bundle of tops and panels and labels. The curtain closes.*)

FATHER TIME. (*stroking his chin*) I'm just wondering if it was all a good idea . . . this postal system. (*He exits shaking his head.*)

SUGGESTIONS

You could eliminate the announcer here if you want to. Any of the lines you wish to keep about the postal service could be given to Father Time. By the way, a long curled paper beard, a staff, and a sheet will be costume enough for the old fellow. He tells the audience who he is anyhow.

The caveman would be ideal in skins or something that looks like skins, if possible, but burlap will do. Smudge up his face with charcoal, rumple his hair, and give him a club. The rock can be a chair covered with paper in such a way that the sketch can be drawn on it and can be seen at least reasonably well by the audience.

Herodotus is, of course, a Greek. A tunic out of sheeting, plus sandals and a headband will be enough to characterize him.

The western scene can be as simple as you wish, as long as you have a Postmaster or U. S. Mail sign. A counter is suggested in the script, but you could manage without it. Don't forget the mail bag, the long underwear, and the off-stage noises. Have you got someone who can whinny like a horse? No one calls Dirty Dan by name, and the fact that he sneaks out when the poster is put up should indicate that he is the one wanted. If it is possible to have a drawing which resembles Dan, that would be fine.

Do what you wish with the lonely heart's gal. She should be ridiculously homely. How about a witch's mask left over from Halloween or one with buck teeth and a bulbous nose. Overdress her too. A great hat with feathers, a long skirt, and let her carry an enormous handbag and a parasol.

For the final scene with the boys get as many cereal boxes as you can. The more there are, the funnier the skit will be. And remember that the things the boys send for should be changed to fit the current fads. You know what they are.

PART VI

THE PLAY

THE PLAY

. . . altogether now . . .

This is what you've been building up to—the one-act play. Although the sketch required each actor to think of the show as a whole and to cooperate with fellow players, there is even greater responsibility in these areas now. The play is longer. There are more lines to learn. The action is more involved.

Still, by the time you undertake a play, the responsibility is accepted as a matter of course. Being heard, memorizing lines, speaking on cue should all be easier and not the main concern. Attention can be directed instead to giving personality to the characters, conviction to the dialogue, realism to the situations. You will create a make-believe world and carry your audience along with you.

Prepare to take a bow.

CALLYOPE, THE CRYING COMIC

CHARACTERS

RINGMASTER, THE NARRATOR
MR. BONE, THE OWNER OF THE CIRCUS, GUARDIAN OF CALLYOPE
CALLYOPE, THE CRYING COMIC
MR. PLOTZ, THE FAT MAN
BERTIE, THE TWO-HEADED BOY
HERCULES, THE STRONG MAN
THE MIDGET
THE BOY

The scene is laid in a section of the circus grounds. The exit, stage left, is into the wagon where CALLYOPE *and* MR. BONE *live. The rest of the stage can be as simply or as elaborately designed as desired. There is a camp stool beside the wagon exit. The curtain does not open at once. The* RINGMASTER *steps outside the curtain and to the far right.*

RINGMASTER. Once upon a time there was a circus. It was almost like every other circus. There were the elephants and the lions. There were the acrobats and the trapeze artists and the bareback riders on their fine Arabian horses. There was the circus band, too, and the side show, and the clowns. But most of all there was Callyope, the crying comic. . . . Callyope was more than just a clown. *He* was the circus. And people came from all over the country just to see him cry. (CALLYOPE *steps through the center parting of the curtain if there is one; otherwise he steps in front of the curtain from the wings.*) He started out with a sigh (CALLYOPE *matches his actions to the* RINGMASTER*'s words*), then he sniffled, then he squeezed out a sob, and finally the tears started to roll down his cheeks. Callyope worked himself up to the very best crying anybody ever heard. And he was so funny that people had to hold their sides they laughed so hard. There is no question about it, crying was Callyope's specialty. Actually he didn't do anything else. He didn't talk much . . . or sing . . . or do any tricks. And what was more, he never laughed. In fact that was the thing that started all the trouble. He didn't know how to laugh. (CALLYOPE *exits crying.*) And it was all because of Mr. Bone.

(*Curtain opens on circus ground scene.* MR. BONE *is sitting on the stool outside the entrance to his wagon. He is whittling at an old branch.* CALLYOPE *enters right and crosses to his guardian.*)

CALLYOPE. Look, Mr. Bone, I caught a grasshopper . . . just with my bare hands. Isn't he funny looking?

MR. BONE. (*knocking it out of his hand*) Let it go, boy. Let it go. You got no time to fritter away with grasshoppers.

CALLYOPE. But I do have time, Mr. Bone. I'm on my way now to find Bertie. We're gonna feed peanuts to the elephants.

MR. BONE. Oh, no you ain't. You go feedin' peanuts to the elephants then there'd be nothin' for the customers to do. You leave them elephants alone, boy.

CALLYOPE. If you say so, Mr. Bone. (*his face lights up*) I know what I can do. I'll climb that tree just outside the circus grounds.

MR. BONE. Climb a tree, eh! Why we can't have that, boy . . .

CALLYOPE. I saw somebody up there in the branches yesterday. He was watching the show, and it looked like great fun.

MR. BONE. What's that you say . . . watching the show. I'll put a stop to that. We'll have no watchers that ain't paid watchers. You just tell me if you see that boy there again.

CALLYOPE. (*sighs*) O.K. I'll just find Mr. Plotz. He said when I had some free time he'd teach me to pla . . . (*he changes the word*) shoot marbles.

MR. BONE. Free time! Free time! You got no free time, boy. You got to work hard. Fun and free time ain't for you.

CALLYOPE. But Mr. Hercules says . . .

MR. BONE. Now you lookie here, boy, don't you mind what Hercules says. You just tell me who it was found you in a basket on his doorstep when you was no bigger than a weasel?

CALLYOPE. Why it was you, Mr. Bone.

MR. BONE. Right you are. And who was it raised you up to be the greatest attraction under that old big top?

CALLYOPE. You, of course, Mr. Bone.

MR. BONE. Then don't let me hear no more talk about grasshoppers or marbles or feedin' the elephants or climbin' trees. Now you just sit down here with your free time, and I'll tell you a story.

CALLYOPE. But I don't want to hear a story, Mr. Bone.

MR. BONE. You don't hardly know what you want, boy. Now you just sit there and listen. You see once there was this little kid . . . name of Elmer. He lived way up on the top floor of this big building. And his ma went away every day, and she locked the door so's he couldn't get out. Now Elmer he didn't have no books, nor no television, nor even no toys. He just sat there day after day thinkin' how miserable he was. Well, sir, he got so desperate he went to the window which was sixty-two floors above the street, and he climbed right out on the ledge . . .

CALLYOPE. I don't want to hear no more, Mr. Bone. (*All through the story* CALLYOPE *is working up to cry. At this point he is in good form.*)

MR. BONE. O.K. boy, now you just run off to bed. And you cry yourself to sleep good. There's an afternoon show tomorrow.

(CALLYOPE *exits into the wagon, and* MR. BONE *watches him off. Then he crosses the stage and exits right.*)

RINGMASTER. Now the only real friends Callyope had were the people of the side show. They loved him very much, and they didn't think it was right that he didn't laugh like other boys. There was Mr. Plotz, the fat man. There was Hercules, who could lift 839½ pounds with one hand. There was Bertie, the boy with two heads, but I'm almost sure one of them wasn't real. And there was the midget. And every once in awhile they had a conference about poor Callyope.

(*As the* RINGMASTER *mentions the members of the side show they enter from various spots onto the stage and gather together.*)

PLOTZ. Have you seen Callyope today? He looks sadder than ever.

BERTIE. I told him a funny joke yesterday, but he didn't even smile.

HERCULES. That doesn't surprise me. Your jokes wouldn't make me smile either.

PLOTZ. I just wish he'd been left at my doorstep, that's all.

MIDGET. I still say we have to make him laugh. Somehow. He can't go on like this. He'll just die of a broken heart.

BERTIE. Here he comes now. I've got another good joke for him. (CALLYOPE *enters.*) Hello there, Callyope. Did you hear about the big fight on the train last night. Do you know what happened?

(CALLYOPE *shakes his head.*)

BERTIE. The conductor punched the ticket, that's what. (*laughs*)

CALLYOPE. (*sniffles*) That's too bad . . . too bad.

(HERCULES *groans at the old joke.*)

MIDGET. Your stories are pretty bad. Let me try. Look, Callyope, let me tell you about the reporter who went to the circus to interview Tom Thumb. Well, the circus manager says, "Tom's not here on Mondays, but you can find him down at the hotel where he lives." The reporter went down to the hotel, found the fellow's room, and knocked. This man about six feet tall came to the door, and the reporter says, "I'd like to see Tom Thumb." "I'm Tom Thumb," says the big guy. And the reporter kinda laughed and says, "No, I mean the little guy, Tom Thumb, the midget." The six-footer, he just stood his ground. "That's me," he says. "This is my day off."

(MIDGET *laughs and* CALLYOPE *keeps on crying.*)

PLOTZ. I might know you'd get in a commercial, but that story's worse than Bertie's.

BERTIE. I'll say. I don't even understand it.

RINGMASTER. (*to the audience*) That joke is a little confusing. Did you get it?

HERCULES. Telling stories isn't going to do any good. Let me have a go at it my way. Look, Callyope, you want to be happy, don't you?

CALLYOPE. (*through his tears*) Yes.

HERCULES. Well, when people are happy they laugh. Like all the boys and girls that come to the big tent to see you. Now I want you to try real hard. First, you think of something good . . .

MIDGET. Like your mother.

HERCULES. That won't do. He doesn't have a mother. Now you just stay out of this. (*He pushes the* MIDGET *aside.*) Start again. You think of something real good like buttered popcorn and cotton candy. Then you think of something very funny like the spider monkey over in the animal tent . . . the one that swings by his tail and squirts water at the ladies. Then you turn up the corners of your mouth like this (*he demonstrates*), and then you let out a happy, happy, sound. Try real hard, now. (*All laugh except* CALLYOPE.) Keep trying . . .

BERTIE. Remember the popcorn!

MIDGET. And the cotton candy!

PLOTZ. And the monkey!

(CALLYOPE *almost smiles, and then it turns to a frown and he cries.*)

BERTIE. Now what's the matter?

MIDGET. Wasn't the cotton candy good?

CALLYOPE. It blew away.

BERTIE. How about the popcorn?

CALLYOPE. The monkey grabbed it, and then he ran off too.

(*They all end up crying and exit in great commotion.*)

RINGMASTER. Well, that's the way it went. The side show people decided that something drastic had to be done. But one night . . . (*lights gradually dim leaving only the night lights of the circus grounds*) Callyope took matters in his own hands. He slipped out of Mr. Bone's wagon and ran away. He ran and ran and ran until at last he was so tired he curled up and went to sleep.

(If possible it is most effective to have CALLYOPE *slip out of the wagon, down off the front of the stage, around to the back of the theater and return to curl up on the stage just in front of the curtain line. After* CALLYOPE *has left the stage,* MR. BONE *pokes his head out of the wagon. He is in nightshirt and cap, and he has a flashlight. He starts across the stage.)*

MR. BONE. Callyope! Callyope!

RINGMASTER. There was a great commotion at the circus when Callyope's absence was discovered. Mr. Bone was furious, and the side show people were quite frightened.

(HERCULES, PLOTZ, BERTIE, *and the* MIDGET *all enter carrying flashlights.)*

MR. BONE. That ungrateful boy. This is the thanks I get for making him famous. Everything I done for him . . . everything to keep him unhappy and successful.

PLOTZ. I wonder where he's gone.

MR. BONE. To catch grasshoppers more'n likely.

PLOTZ. I hope somebody will teach him to play marbles.

HERCULES. And climb trees.

MIDGET. And laugh.

BERTIE. Oh, I do hope somebody can make him laugh.

(MR. BONE *storms back and forth waving his flash-light.*)

MR. BONE. Laugh! Laugh! I'll teach you to laugh out of that second head of yours if we don't find him. Hear that now.

PLOTZ. Poor Callyope.

MR. BONE. Poor Callyope! Poor Bone you best say. And poor circus. There just ain't any circus without that miserable boy. Heads up now. Keep a weather eye. Mr. Bone will bring him back. (*He starts toward exit at the right of the stage.*)

MIDGET. Like that! (*He points to pantless Bone and* MR. BONE, *suddenly aware of his garb, scowls and storms back to the wagon and exits as the others laugh.*)

BERTIE. I'll bet that would have made Callyope laugh. (*Thinking of* CALLYOPE, *they are all sad again.*)

PLOTZ. If Mr. Bone finds him, it won't help matters. If there was only something *we* could do.

HERCULES. You ought to be able to think of something, Bertie. Two heads are better than one.

BERTIE. (*scratching both his heads*) *We* could look for him *ourselves.*

MIDGET. Yes, but if we brought him back he'd still have to live with Mr. Bone, and he'd go right on crying.

PLOTZ. That's right. He's better off lost. But I'm afraid the circus is lost too.

(*They all exit as they came in as the curtain closes.*)

RINGMASTER. Well, they all decided Plotz was right. Callyope was better off lost. Even if the circus wasn't the same. But Mr. Bone kept on looking for him. He looked for a long, long time. (*As* MR. BONE *goes through the theater with his flashlight,* CALLYOPE *wakes up and takes a bag of peanuts from his pocket. There are no elephants to feed them to so he just munches on them himself. He looks dejected.*) Of course, he didn't find him. But somebody did. (*The* RINGMASTER *shades his eyes to watch the* BOY *who comes down to the stage from the back of the theater.*) It was a boy, and he looked just about as miserable as Callyope.

(*The* BOY, *who is crying, mounts the steps and moves toward* CALLYOPE.)

CALLYOPE. Say there! What's the matter? Why are *you* crying?

THE BOY. You wouldn't care.

CALLYOPE. Oh, yes I would. Crying is my specialty.

THE BOY. Well, I saved a penny a day for two-hundred-and-thirty-one days so that I could go to the circus. I wanted to get pink lemonade and cotton candy and popcorn and ride on the merry-go-round and see the side show. But most of all I wanted to see Callyope. (*He stops to cry.*) But now, there isn't any circus.

CALLYOPE. There is so a circus. You can even see the big top from here. (*He stands up and points far over to the right.*) And if you listen real hard you can hear the lions roar.

(*They listen and there is a faint sound.*)

THE BOY. Oh, the tent's there all right, and the animals and the cotton candy and the pink lemonade. The side show's there too, but it's in terrible shape. You see Callyope's gone, and Callyope is the real circus. You'd cry too, if you were me.

CALLYOPE. I can cry even if I'm not you. (*thinks about it all and starts to cry according to his usual procedure*)

THE BOY. Now wait a minute. You cry like . . . you must be . . . why you *are* Callyope. Why did you run away?

CALLYOPE. I don't know whether you can understand. I wanted to catch grasshoppers and climb a tree and feed the elephants and learn to play marbles. And most of all I wanted to laugh. Mr. Bone wouldn't let me.

THE BOY. Mr. Bone?

CALLYOPE. He's my guardian. It's his circus.

THE BOY. He's gone too. Out looking for you. (*thinks a bit*) I'll tell you what. If I can make you laugh, will you go back to the circus with me?

CALLYOPE. If you can make me laugh, I'll do anything. But I warn you it isn't going to be easy. You'd have to be a magician.

THE BOY. Well, I just may have a little magic. (*He fumbles in his pocket, apparently finds what he's looking for but doesn't take it out.*) I was sure I had it with me. Now you just listen to me while we head back to the circus. (*They start back around the theater on their return to the stage. The* BOY *talks as he goes.*) The circus is just going to pieces. Mr. Bone is out hunting for you. The elephants won't eat . . . not even peanuts. The pink lemonade is sour. Nobody will drink it. The band is all out of tune. And the side show . . . wait till you see . . . (*His voice dwindles away as the curtain opens and the* RINGMASTER *speaks again.*)

RINGMASTER. That's right. The circus is going to pieces. Mr. Plotz has lost so much weight people won't even pay to see him. Hercules has been worrying so he hasn't the strength to lift even a feather let alone 839½ pounds. The midget . . . well, he's started to grow. And as for Bertie . . . what has happened to him is almost too sad to tell.

(*By this time* CALLYOPE *and the* BOY *are back on the steps of the stage watching as the side show people enter, changed as indicated.* BERTIE *has no head at all.*)

PLOTZ. I don't know what's to become of us. I can't eat. I try. (*He munches on a sandwich in his hands.*) But it sticks in my throat.

HERCULES. Look at me. I'm a nervous wreck. I shake so I can't even lift a Ping-Pong ball let alone a weight.

MIDGET. You should talk. What am I to do? If I grow any taller, I won't *be* a midget. I'll be kicked out of the union. I'll lose my identity.

BERTIE. (*voice from neck of coat*) Well, I'm the most wretched of all. Who ever heard of a two-headed boy with *no* heads. I'm a disgrace to my whole family. I'm ruined.

(CALLYOPE *has been building up to a good cry all this time, and as he reaches the peak of his performance the* BOY *takes a mirror from his pocket.*)

THE BOY. Now . . . now . . . Callyope. Look at yourself . . . look in the mirror.

(CALLYOPE *sees himself in the mirror and slowly his crying changes. He smiles. He chuckles. He finally laughs with great gusto.*)

CALLYOPE. I'm laughing! I'm laughing! It's the most wonderful feeling in the world.

THE BOY. Come on, Callyope. Let's go to the circus. (*They exit into the wings and enter onto the circus grounds at upstage left.* CALLYOPE *is still laughing.*)

PLOTZ, HERCULES, MIDGET. (*together*) That looks like Callyope.

BERTIE. It doesn't sound like Callyope. I know laughter when I hear it.

THE BOY. Oh, it's Callyope, all right.

PLOTZ. You've saved the circus.

MIDGET. Looks more like you saved Callyope.

THE BOY. But he isn't going to cry any more.

PLOTZ, MIDGET, HERCULES. Hurrah for Callyope!

(MR. BONE *enters from the right. He's haggard and stooped and has apparently aged.*)

MR. BONE. Callyope, eh. Did I hear someone mention Callyope?

HERCULES. It's Mr. Bone come back. You'd better hide, Callyope.

MR. BONE. Ho there now, boy. (*holds up the flashlight he is still carrying*) I been lookin' for you . . . been lookin' for you till I'm plumb wore out. Reckon you forgot who found you in that basket and raised you up successful. Eh?

CALLYOPE. I sure never did forget that, Mr. Bone.

BERTIE. He'll make you cry again, Callyope. Please hide.

MR. BONE. Cry! That's the thing. Got to get back in form, boy.

PLOTZ. Oh dear. He'll have him right back where he was before.

MR. BONE. (*ignores* PLOTZ) Reckon I got things to say'll make you cry, all right. (*He takes a step toward* CALLYOPE.)

MIDGET. Don't do it, Mr. Bone. Things are bad enough as they are. The side show's a mess. Just look at us.

THE BOY. (*crosses to* BONE) Don't you come a step closer, Mr. Bone. You left your circus, and I don't think anybody missed you a bit. (*turning to* CALLYOPE) Don't you be unhappy, Callyope.

CALLYOPE. Unhappy! Nobody should be unhappy when they know how to laugh. I'm not going to be unhappy ever again.

MR. BONE. We'll see about that . . . (*moves toward* CALLYOPE *again*) You'll do whatever I say, Callyope. Remember how I found you and raised you up.

MIDGET. You keep saying that, Mr. Bone, but Hercules is the one who found Callyope beside your wagon. And Bertie was the one that named him. And Mr. Plotz and I took care of him when he was a little mite. All you did was put him to work as soon as you taught him how to cry.

HERCULES. That's right, Mr. Bone.

BERTIE and PLOTZ. Right . . . that's right.

THE BOY. In that case I think there should be a conference. (*He motions Callyope's friends to stage right where they whisper.*)

CALLYOPE. (*at stage left with* BONE) Is that true, Mr. Bone? You didn't really find me after all?

(BONE *grudgingly nods as the conference breaks up.*)

THE BOY. We have come to a decision. I brought Callyope back to the circus, but I'm not going to let him stay. In fact I'm taking everybody away with me. We'll start a new circus.

(*They start to exit.*)

MR. BONE. You can't do that to poor old Bone. Tell them you won't leave me, Callyope. Look, I'm begging you. (*He gets on his knees.*)

CALLYOPE. Wait a minute. You know I do feel kind of sorry for him.

THE BOY. I don't see how you can, but I guess we could find another way. (*The group confers again. Then the* BOY *turns to* BONE.) Mr. Bone. There are conditions. You must first apologize to Callyope.

MR. BONE. Oh, I do. I do. (*He wrings his hands.*)

THE BOY. And half the circus will belong to Callyope because of all the back pay you owe him.

MR. BONE. (*hesitates and the* BOY *starts to leave again*) All right if I have to . . . anything to save my circus.

THE BOY. That's not all. Since you were the one who made Callyope cry, you must now do something to make him laugh . . . at *every performance.*

MR. BONE. How can I ever do that? I can't even laugh myself.

THE BOY. We'll find a way. (*turns to nod to the others*)

MR. BONE. All right, I promise.

THE BOY. Very well, then everything will turn out all right. The circus will be better than ever.

CALLYOPE. I'll say it will. And look, Mr. Plotz is hungry already.

(PLOTZ *has found the sandwich he was trying to eat earlier. He had put it in his pocket. The curtain closes.*)

RINGMASTER. Well, that's the way it turned out. In no time at all things got back to normal. The midget stopped growing just in time. Hercules got his strength back in three days, and on the fourth day he was able to lift 839 and ¾ pounds. Mr. Plotz gained weight so fast he had to go on a diet. And Bertie . . . well you'll have to see him to believe it. (BERTIE *enters with three heads.*) Now the circus is almost like every other circus. There are the acrobats and the trapeze artists and the bareback riders on their Arabian horses. There is the circus band and the side show. And there are the clowns too. But most of all there is Callyope. And Callyope *is* the circus. He doesn't cry any more though. He just laughs. It's his specialty. People come from all over the country just to hear him. First he smiles, and then he chuckles, and then he bursts out in such glee that tears roll down his cheeks. And he works up to the very best merriment that anybody has ever heard. He's so funny that the people laugh until they have to hold their sides. As for Mr. Bone, he's really the one that starts Callyope's laughter. Of course he needs a little push now and then . . .

(*The curtain opens. Everyone is on stage, and* MR. BONE *dressed as a clown is being pushed and shoved by all in turn. He falls down, gets up, falls down again.* CALLYOPE, *watching him, starts to smile and then goes on into his laughter routine.*)

SUGGESTIONS

Callyope can actually be performed on a bare stage. Even the stool Mr. Bone uses could be eliminated. And that gives you more time and energy to devote to the costumes *and* the acting.

The side show characters really provide the challenge. You can put Hercules in sweat suit pants, but the top should be something more tight fitting. You want to be able to pad the arms to make muscles. Then of course the pads are removed when he loses his strength. Mr. Plotz can be stuffed and unstuffed in the same way. The midget should naturally be the smallest actor you have, and when he grows, give him a shorter pair of pants and a shirt with shorter sleeves. One way you can get a second (and a third) head for Bertie is with cotton-stuffed paper bags. Or how about Styrofoam balls, covered with muslin and painted. Of course, they won't look real. Does it matter? The ringmaster himself says he's almost sure the second head isn't real. Then when Bertie loses his head, he just props his coat up from his shoulders and lets his voice float up through the neck.

Hopefully you can put your ringmaster in top hat, boots, and a snappy coat. Any touches you can add to get the feeling of the circus grounds will be fine.

HERE LIES McLEAN

CHARACTERS

THE NARRATOR

PETER HAGGETT, THE CARETAKER OF PARADISE CEMETERY

EMMA HAGGETT, HIS WIFE

LIZZIE KELLY, THE TOWN BUSYBODY OUT TO CATCH A MAN

LUKE THOMAS, THE MAN, ALSO THE UNDERTAKER OF TABOR CITY

HORATIO, THE ACTOR

MC LEAN, ???

The scene is laid in the front room of the caretaker's cottage. There is a door at center back which leads outside. It is equipped with several bolts, none of which are fastened. To the left of the door there is a window with a small table and a chair in front of it. On the table are several flowering plants and a telephone. Upstage on the left wall is a bookcase or cupboard holding, among other things, a few cups and a large alarm clock, which has stopped at 12:30. Farther downstage on the same wall is a door which leads to the rest of the house. There is a second window on the right stage wall with a chair beside it, and a third door downstage right which also leads outside. This door has a single chain bolt, but it too is unlatched. At right center is a table strewn with newspapers and with three straight chairs drawn up to it. The

NARRATOR *enters in front of the closed curtain and takes a place at the right.*

NARRATOR. Our play tonight is about ghosts and graveyards and faces at the window and about Emma Haggett who is unhappy with all of them. You see, Peter Haggett, her husband, is the caretaker of Paradise Cemetery, and he spends so much time out there taking care that Emma is lonely . . . and she's scared too. She gets away from the place as much as she can, and tonight Lizzie Kelly and Luke Thomas, who runs the funeral parlor in Tabor City, took her to town to see a traveling show company perform *Hamlet*. You know about Hamlet—the prince that talks to his father's ghost. But I'm telling too much of the story. They've just come back from the play now. Let's see what happens.

> (*The* NARRATOR *steps back into the wings. The curtain opens and* EMMA, LIZZIE, *and* LUKE *enter from the door on the right.*)

EMMA. Well, here we are. (*She crosses to the door on the left and calls out.*) Peter! We're back. (*She puts her hat and coat on the chair by the window on the back wall, and when she sees the unbolted center door she hurries over to fasten all of the locks.*)

LIZZIE. You've put on another bolt, haven't you, Em? (*She takes off her coat, putting it around her shoulders.*)

EMMA. No, but I'm going to. And I'm going to have window shades too. (*She looks out the back window, fear-*

fully.) It's so dark out there. (*She turns to* LUKE *who still stands at the right door.*) Lock that door, too, Luke. (LUKE *does as she asks and* EMMA *sighs.*) There, now I feel better. In the daytime I don't mind, but at night . . . (*She sees* LIZZIE *about to take one of the chairs at the table.*) Don't take that chair, Lizzie; the leg's broken. Peter means to fix it. (LIZZIE *pulls up one of the other chairs and sits.*) You'll stay for a cup of tea, won't you?

LUKE. (*still standing*) We ought to be going. It's pretty late.

EMMA. (*heads for the left door which leads off to the kitchen and the rest of the house, calling back over her shoulder*) It won't take a minute. The kettle's on the back of the stove.

(*She exits.* LUKE *takes the other safe chair at the table and hangs his jacket over the back of it.*)

LIZZIE. (*pointing to the alarm and speaking so that* EMMA *can hear*) Is that the right time? It can't be that late.

EMMA. (*entering again, turns the clock over on its face*) No, it's stopped. Peter hasn't fixed that either. I wonder where he is?

LIZZIE. Out tending his graves, I suppose.

LUKE. Well, Peter takes his work serious. He's been caretaker of Paradise for thirty years.

EMMA. (*she has been getting cups from the shelf*) Twenty-nine years, three months, and two days.

LIZZIE. You take your work at the funeral parlor serious too, Luke, but you don't spend your time holding your customers' hands.

EMMA. (*changing the subject*) It was nice of you to take me to the show tonight . . . even though I didn't understand it much.

LIZZIE. *Hamlet* is a real thoughty play, Em. Shakespeare, you know. We don't often get Shakespeare in Tabor City. (EMMA *exits for tea.*)

LUKE. We don't often get a show of any kind. And when we do it's just for one night.

EMMA. (*comes back in with the teapot*) You know I couldn't get used to those grown men traipsing around the stage in long underwear.

LIZZIE. Tights, Em.

EMMA. And it was sad. That poor fellow in black, his pa dead and all. I cried. But that nice young man in the purple underwear. He was a real good friend. What was his name now?

LUKE. Horatio. You know, Em, it was the part about the ghost that Lizzie was afraid you wouldn't like.

(*There is a rattling at the door at the center back.* EMMA *gets behind* LIZZIE*'s chair.* LUKE *goes to unfasten the locks and* PETER *enters.*)

PETER. Dag nab it, a man can't even get in his own house. Hello, Luke . . . Lizzie. (PETER *removes his jacket and cap and tosses them on top of* EMMA*'s coat.*) I knew you were back when I found the door bolted.

EMMA. Peter, you know that door leads right down to the graves. I can't help it if I'm scared.

LIZZIE. Peter, why don't you give up this place? Your business isn't very good anyhow.

PETER. We make out. One thing we got no noisy neighbors. And when the time comes, we got a choice shaded lot out there in the north corner.

LIZZIE. Small comfort to know you're going to be in the shade when you're dead and buried.

PETER. (*as* EMMA *turns her back to the others and puts her hands over her ears*) Well, it's a comfort to me to know I won't be planted alongside you, Lizzie. You'd talk me right up outa the ground.

LIZZIE. All the same, Em needs some living folks around her. You two should move to town to spend your remaining years.

PETER. Remaining years! Now you're talking me into my grave. I may have my spot picked out, but I ain't ready for it yet. Course I do wish business was a little better.

LUKE. The thing is you can't count on local folks only, Peter. You got to reach out. I take care of the whole county, even outside.

PETER. I guess you're right.

EMMA. (*turns around again; once more changing the subject*) Can I give someone some more tea?

LUKE. I'm afraid we have to go, Em. Thanks all the same. (*He gets up.*)

LIZZIE. (*getting up too*) Well, I still say Em ought to get away from here.

EMMA. (*follows them to the door*) Good-by, Lizzie . . . Luke. Thanks again for taking me to the show.

(PETER *adds his good-bys but does not go to the door.* EMMA *closes and bolts the door after* LIZZIE *and* LUKE *leave.*)

PETER. Dag nab Lizzie Kelly. She's nothing but trouble. Trying to get me to leave here so's Luke could take over. She figures he'd be so grateful he'd marry her.

EMMA. You really think that's so, Peter? Luke doesn't need Paradise. His business is good.

PETER. Well, if he was to combine undertaking and burying, he'd sorta have his bread buttered on both sides. (*He is thoughtful for a moment.*) You know his business is good though. And I been thinking. You know it's because he advertises! (PETER *picks up a piece of the newspaper from the table.*) Look here, right on the back page of the *Daily Bugler* . . . every week regular. "Take your last ride with me." Advertising is what Paradise needs! (*pauses*) And Peter Haggett is the man to get it.

EMMA. You can't advertise for no bodies.

PETER. A good burying is what we need all the same . . . a good burying to let folks know we're still here. And I'll get a body if I have to . . . (*He raises his fist to strike the table.*)

EMMA. (*interrupting*) Peter Haggett, you wouldn't dare!

(*There is a quick curtain as the* NARRATOR *enters again from the wings.*)

NARRATOR. We just closed the curtain there for a minute so that you'll know that time has gone by. It is midnight of the next day. Notice that the side door's bolted, but the one that leads down to the graves isn't. And watch the windows. Watch the windows. (*The* NARRATOR *exits.*)

(*As the curtain opens,* EMMA *enters nervously from the left. She wears a big flannel nightgown and floppy bedroom slippers. She peers out the window at the back. There is a knock at the side door and then there is a tapping at the side window.* EMMA *stands stiff with terror as a face appears. She runs off through the door at the left. The face appears again at the back window and then disappears.* PETER *enters through the back center door. He is dressed as before and carries a shovel which he stands against the wall.*)

PETER. (*shivers and rubs his hands together to warm them*) Dag nab it, it's cold out there. (*calls out*) Em, you awake?

EMMA. (*enters from left*) Thank heaven you're back. There was someone at the window, Peter. I saw him. (*She points to the window on the right wall.*)

PETER. (*crosses to the window and looks out*) Ain't nothing out there, Em. Ain't you been asleep?

EMMA. How could I sleep with the back door unbolted, and you out there on such business?

PETER. Now Em, I ain't done nothing. (*He locks the back door.*)

EMMA. You call this Alexander McLean business nothing? It's sinful, that's what it is.

PETER. You talk like McLean was real. I made him up. You know there ain't nothing out there in that grave. We needed a burying and that's what we got. A fine grave with a three-foot gravestone on it. It's been a long time since I cut a stone. "Alexander X. McLean . . . A Nobler Man You Never Seen." It came out real good, and if you weren't such a scaredy you'd been out there with me. You ain't mad I took our lot, are you? There's another just as good on the south side.

EMMA. It ain't the lot, Peter. I just don't see how this thing's going to do any good. And I still say it's sinful.

PETER. Don't you worry. I got it all figured out. But I'll tell you about it tomorrow. I'm tired.

(PETER *and* EMMA *exit. After they are gone there is a tapping at the back window and the face appears again. The audience gets a good look at* HORATIO, *who is, of course, the one outside. The curtain closes and the* NARRATOR *steps from the wings.*)

NARRATOR. Peter had it all figured out all right. And it was pretty good. The next morning he'd go to town to put a notice in the *Daily Bugler*. Alexander McLean came in on the night train from Wood River. He had it in his will that he was to be buried at Paradise, a private service at the stroke of midnight. You see, Peter's brother has the freight office, and he promised that that was all the information he'd give out if anyone checked the story. And Peter can trust his brother. Now while Peter was in town Emma was busy with her morning work. She got her bread in the oven and dusted up the living room and then . . .

(*The curtain opens and the* NARRATOR *steps offstage. There is a loud knocking at the back door which is now unbolted.* EMMA, *who is not as afraid in the daytime, opens the door to find* HORATIO. *He looks as though he has slept in his clothes and he carries an old battered suitcase.*)

HORATIO. (*with a sweeping bow*) Dear lady, may I have a word with you? (*As he steps inside* EMMA *recognizes the face and she backs away a little.*) It was you I saw at the window last night. . . . What do you want?

HORATIO. I repeat, dear lady, just a word. (*He smells the baking bread.*) Sweet smell of heaven. That must be homemade bread.

EMMA. It is. Now what's your name?

HORATIO. (*as though reciting*) Horatio, friend of Hamlet.

EMMA. (*remembering the play*) You're one of those actor fellows from the show. Horatio—the one with the purple underwear. Well, I say this, you were a nice young man in that play.

HORATIO. (*moves into the room with his suitcase*) And therein lies my problem. So exhausted was I with being a friend I fell asleep out in the meadow behind the playhouse, and the show moved on without me. Here I am stranded and without a penny.

(*He puts his suitcase down and before* EMMA *can stop him he sits in the broken chair which collapses with him.*)

EMMA. I'm sorry. I should have warned you.

HORATIO. (*as though nothing happened he goes on talking from the floor*) I was wondering, dear lady, if there might be some odd jobs I could do to fend off starvation and get me back to Hamlet. (*smells the bread again*) Oh, that bread. (*rises*) By the way what was the old man doing out there with the shovel at midnight?

EMMA. (*a little worried now*) You seen Peter then. Look here, you've no call to make trouble, have you?

HORATIO. Trouble! I'd just like to get out of my own trouble. (*then deciding to flatter her a bit*) What I really want to know is why a lovely lady like you is in an eerie place like this.

EMMA. (*reacting to the flattery she tucks in the straggling ends of her hair*) You are a nice young man. (*She looks him over.*) I have chicken money enough to pay for a few chores. I don't need to tell Peter. And maybe if you're handy with a hammer you'll fix the leg on that chair. You might even fix my clock. And you look hungry. . . . Oh, I'd best get the bread out before it burns.

(EMMA *exits, and as* HORATIO *inspects the chair she calls from offstage.*)

EMMA. Wait now, and I'll have something for you to eat. (*reenters with the bread, a knife, and a pitcher of milk*) Well, I'll tell you. Peter had a funeral out there last night. He buried this McLean out in the north corner, and he didn't want anyone to know about it.

HORATIO. You can't very well hide a grave . . . not if someone really wants to find it.

EMMA. Oh, it isn't the grave he's trying to hide. It's the body. I mean . . . it isn't the body exactly either . . . what I mean to say is this McLean ain't alive.

HORATIO. I hope not. If he's buried in the north corner.

EMMA. I know it don't make much sense, but you see there's no body there. McLean's just made up.

HORATIO. I see. A figment of the imagination.

EMMA. Peter figures that if Paradise gets a piece in the paper now and then it will bring him a little business.

HORATIO. Nothing wrong with that. So Peter dreams up a corpse. Who cares?

EMMA. I'll tell you who cares. Lizzie Kelly. If Lizzie knew about this she'd have everybody laughing at Peter. And them as didn't laugh would say Peter was meddling with the Almighty. And when they run him out of town, she'd move in. I think Peter's right. Lizzie wants Luke and she wants Paradise. And I wish she had them both.

HORATIO. If you wish she had Paradise, dear lady, why don't you just tell Lizzie what went on last night?

EMMA. I couldn't go against my man, young fellow. I shouldn't even be telling you, but I had to talk to somebody.

HORATIO. Your secret is as safe with me as it is with McLean, dear lady. I consider my promise to you a grave responsibility.

EMMA. (*listens*) I think I hear the car. Slip out the side door. You'll find an old barn down the road where you can stay. Every morning when Peter goes into town, you come up over the field and I'll find some work for you to do . . . I'll feed you too.

HORATIO. I shall be indebted to you for all my days, dear lady. This bread (*he takes another slice*) is fit for a king. (*He bows and exits.*)

(EMMA, *who hasn't had a compliment in years, hums a little tune and dances around the room. Then she gathers up the bread and milk, and as she exits left* PETER *comes in the back door.*)

PETER. (*calls out*) Em! (EMMA *reenters.*) Well, it went off real good. Only bad luck I had was running into Lizzie. She followed me right to the *Bugler* office, but she didn't hear nothing but what I told the paper. That woman is the nosiest. (PETER *hears something outside and looks out the right window.*) Well, I'll be dag nabbed, if that ain't Lizzie out there now. How do you suppose she got here so quick?

(*There is a knock and* EMMA *crosses to open the door.* LIZZIE *enters.*)

LIZZIE. If you'd waited I'd a rode home with you, Peter. Thank goodness I got a ride with the postman. I been just dying to find out about this funeral you had here last night, Em. I couldn't get a thing outa Peter. It must of been kind of inconvenient. A burying at midnight. Queer thing to ask for.

PETER. Yep. It sure was.

LIZZIE. You know I'd a been glad to come out and cry a little over the grave. I wouldn't have minded the hour. I think I'll just step out now and pay my respects.

PETER. I'll show you where it is . . . (*They move to the door.*)

EMMA. Will you stay for supper, Lizzie? I've fresh bread.

LIZZIE. Can't tonight, Em. Luke said he'd pick me up. Some other time. (LIZZIE *and* PETER *exit. Almost at once the phone rings.*)

EMMA. (*answering*) Hello. Oh hello, Luke. Yes, Lizzie's here. I'll tell her. (*She hangs up and calls out the door.*)

Lizzie, that was Luke. He says he's on his way, and he's in a hurry. Wants you to meet him at the crossroads. (EMMA *picks up the clock, looks at it thoughtfully, then puts it down again as* PETER *enters.*)

PETER. Nosey woman. I'm sure glad Luke called. She didn't have time to see it.

EMMA. She'll come back, Peter. Suppose somebody was to find out?

PETER. (*irritated*) Dag nab ya, Em. There's no call to suppose. Lizzie's the only one to worry about, and I could tell she don't know a thing. Can't find out nothing either 'less she goes way up to Wood River. And she won't do that.

EMMA. I just said suppose.

(PETER *has been looking over the plants on the table. He picks out the prettiest flower and starts toward the door.*)

EMMA. Where you goin' with that?

PETER. I'm decorating the grave of Alexander McLean. May the good man rest in peace. (PETER *exits. The curtain closes.*)

NARRATOR. (*entering as before*) It's been a week now since Peter's advertising, and it looks like his fortune has taken a turn for the good. There have been three burials at Paradise in as many days . . . folks from outside the county. Emma, of course, has Horatio to keep her company when Peter goes off to town, and she's changed a little too, but you'll see. It's evening. Emma's alone and . . .

(*The curtain opens.* EMMA *with her hair neater than before and wearing a bright colored apron over her dress enters as there is a knock at the door, right. She opens it cautiously to admit* HORATIO.)

HORATIO. Here's your clock, dear lady. Is it all right for me to come in?

EMMA. Oh yes. Peter's still in town. He said he'd be late. Did you get the clock fixed?

HORATIO. Right here. (*He puts the clock back in its place on the shelf.*) How's the chair holding up?

EMMA. Fine. Peter ain't even noticed.

HORATIO. And now, dear lady, it's time I was moving on.

EMMA. You mean you're going back to the show?

HORATIO. If I can get into my tights. Any more of your wonderful food and I'd never be friend to Hamlet again.

EMMA. It's been real nice having you here.

HORATIO. Well, I'm one fellow that's enjoyed his stay at Paradise.

EMMA. (*sighs*) I wish I could say the same.

HORATIO. You're really unhappy here, aren't you, dear lady?

EMMA. At least, like Peter says, the neighbors aren't noisy.

HORATIO. I'm sorry, really I am. I wish there was something I could do. (*He puts his hands on her shoulders.*) But don't you give up, dear lady. Don't you ever give up. Something will turn up, you'll see.

(HORATIO *steps back, lifts her hand to his lips in the manner of Horatio, the actor. Then he exits.* EMMA *bolts the door behind him, picks up her mending basket.* PETER *calls from the back center door.*)

PETER. Em, it's me. (EMMA *lets him in and* PETER *enters waving letters in his hand.*) Advertising! That's the ticket. These were waiting for me at the post office. One, two, three more requests to be buried at Paradise. It's catching hold. I think in a year or two we'll need more ground.

(EMMA *says nothing all this while, but now she wipes her eyes.*)

PETER. Now, Em, you ain't fixing to cry? Just when things are looking good. You'll get used to it here. You gotta admit there ain't no place prettier in the summer . . . all green and warm.

EMMA. It ain't summer now, Peter. I can't ever get used to the blackness of the night and the queer feeling after the sun goes down.

PETER. You'll feel better about it in the morning. (*He sees the clock.*) Say, ain't that old clock about right? I thought it needed fixing. Looks like everything's decided to run smooth a spell. (*yawns and stretches*) I'm turning in.

EMMA. Well I won't stay out here alone. You get the light.

(EMMA *puts aside her mending.* PETER *turns off the light. The stage dims, and as* PETER *starts toward the back center door there is a knock on it.*)

PETER. Now who do you suppose that is. We don't get callers after dark. (EMMA *moves back toward the left exit, frightened.*) Who's there? (*no answer*) Dag nab ya. Who's there?

(*The door slowly opens and in walks a strange figure. With each step it takes forward,* PETER *takes two back so that finally he is at the far left with* EMMA *hiding behind him. The ghostly figure can either be* HORATIO *himself with a mask and a white sheet that could be put on in the time there is or it could be another actor with a more elaborate costume.*)

MC LEAN. (*in an eerie voice*) Peter Haggett, caretaker of Paradise?

PETER. (*with an effort at bravery*) That's who I am. What do you want? If you're looking for a grave, this is a fine time of . . .

MC LEAN. I'm not looking for a grave. Thanks to you, I have one.

PETER. Who are you?

MC LEAN. You ought to know. I'm McLean . . . Alexander X.

PETER. You can't be.

MC LEAN. I've come from the north corner, Haggett, and it's damp and cold out there. I'm not going to stay.

PETER. Then don't. That's all right with me.

MC LEAN. I'm glad you feel that way. Because I've come to stay here with you. (*He sweeps across the room to seat himself on the chair at the right wall. As he gathers his cape around him, his purple tights are clearly visible.* EMMA, *who sees who it is, pokes* PETER, *but he pushes her hand away.*)

PETER. You can't do that. (*He is terrified.*)

MC LEAN. You'll see, Peter Haggett, you'll see.

EMMA. (*pokes* PETER *again*) Peter . . . Peter . . . I think . . . (PETER *turns to her just as* MC LEAN *shakes his head negatively.* EMMA *claps her hand over her mouth and says no more.*)

PETER. (*in a whisper to* EMMA) Emma, I've made up my mind. Go pack your satchel. We're leaving out the kitchen door.

EMMA. (*in surprise*) You mean you'd leave like this, here and now? Peter Haggett, you're afraid.

PETER. Look here, Em. I ain't afeerd of a living man, and I ain't afeerd of them that's dead and proper buried, but this here McLean never was. I made him up, and he's come to haunt me.

EMMA. You sure, Peter, it's not some trick?

PETER. (*with impatience*) Dab nab ya, Em, I tell ya there's no one to play tricks. Besides have you ever seen the likes of him (*points to* MC LEAN) around these parts before? Have ya now?

EMMA. (*hesitates as* MC LEAN *shakes his head as before*) I guess you're right, Peter. I guess you're right.

(*She exits.* PETER *turns to face* MC LEAN *and then backs out the door.* MC LEAN *is alone on the stage for a moment and then* EMMA *comes back in and reaches for the clock.*)

EMMA. (*a little timidly*) I didn't want to forget my clock. (*pauses*) He really means it. We're leaving Paradise just like this after twenty-nine years. (*She backs up a little as* MC LEAN *rises.*) I just had to say thank you. (*She starts to leave and then turns once again.*) And by the way, there's some chocolate cake in the cupboard.

(*There is a quick curtain as* MC LEAN *makes a deep bow. The* NARRATOR *reenters.*)

NARRATOR. Well, that's the story. Luke and Lizzie did take over Paradise, and once in awhile somebody asks whatever became of the Haggetts. Nobody in Tabor City seems to know, but I can tell you. They are about as far away from Paradise as they could get. Emma is surrounded by living folks, and Peter, who sells hot roasted chestnuts in the park, keeps looking over his shoulder. And he always makes it a point to get home before dark. Oh yes, Horatio finished off the chocolate cake, and when he went back to Hamlet, he could just barely get into his purple underwear. As for McLean . . . I guess he just rests in peace out there in the north corner.

Suggestions

At first glance it seems that *Here Lies McLean* must have the walls of a regular stage set. That would be best, of course. You could manage, however, as long as you have a back curtain with a center opening. The exit is necessary. You might have only one window, and that at the back. A cardboard frame could be pinned to the curtain. The narrator could explain about all the bolts and locks, and the locking and unlocking of the doors could be pantomime. Although the audience would lose the effect of the "face at the window" there would be Emma's fright, and the narrator could tell what she saw.

The props are indicated in the script and shouldn't be difficult to provide.

The costumes and make-up are easy. Peter looks older than he is and wears work clothes. Emma's hair is gray, and she wears cotton housedresses with covering aprons. Remember Lizzie Kelly is trying to catch a man. She will be "dressed up" and maybe wear a big hat with feathers. Why not make Luke a comic strip undertaker with a black suit and a mournful voice? Horatio might wear a suit which has seen better days and a scarf tucked in at the neck instead of a tie. McLean offers many possibilities, especially if the part is taken by someone other than the person who plays Horatio. Do make him scary.

TORKO THE TERRIBLE

CHARACTERS

THE STORYTELLER, FROM THE AGENCY

MARTIN, THE MONSTER MAKER

HIS MOTHER, OFF-STAGE VOICE

TORKO THE TERRIBLE

LISA, THE BLIND GIRL

ROSIE, THE READER WHO ALWAYS CARRIES A KNAPSACK OF BOOKS

THE OTHER CHILDREN: JOE, STUMPY, FLORA, LUCY, SUSIE, AND AS MANY OTHERS AS DESIRED, BOTH ON THE STAGE AND PLANTED IN THE AUDIENCE.

THE MONSTERS: BIGWART, HAGWART, SAGWART, RAGWART, ZONG, AND AS MANY OTHERS AS DESIRED.

When the show is ready to begin, the STORYTELLER, *a gnomelike character wearing a flopping, peaked cap and spectacles comes out in front of the curtain from the right. He brings with him a high stool and a big ledger. After he bows to the audience, he puts down the stool and looks over the crowd.*

STORYTELLER. I'm from the agency. I was sent here to tell you a story. (*very deliberately he climbs up on the stool and opens the ledger*) But it must be the story for today. Now, let's see, this is 19(*current year*). Yes, here it is. (*He runs his finger down the page.*) And this is (*current month*). And finally the ________ day. (*He names the wrong date.*)

ONE OF THE PLAYERS IN THE AUDIENCE. No! That's not right. Today's the (*correct date*).

STORYTELLER. Not right? Are you sure?

ANOTHER PLAYER IN THE AUDIENCE. Of course we're sure. It's the (*correct date*).

STORYTELLER. Fish feathers! (*shakes his head from side to side*) The agency mixed things up again. (*He adjusts his spectacles, turns the page, and finds the proper place.*) Yes, yes, well here it is . . . (*correct date*). (*He reads to himself, mumbling and then looks up with an expression of alarm.*) Oh my warts and wartles! No wonder they didn't tell me. This is the Day of Strange Happenings! The one day in the whole year. (*He closes the ledger with a bang and climbs down from the stool as he continues.*) No day to tell a story. No day for me even to be out. I should be in bed with the covers pulled up over my head. (*He speaks directly out to the audience with an air of foreboding.*) This is a day the stories tell themselves. (*He picks up his stool and tucks his book under his arm.*) Hurry me home . . . hurry me home . . .

(*As he hurries toward the right exit,* MARTIN *enters left with his arms full of boxes and carrying the* TORKO *figure.*)

MARTIN. Hey, where you going in such a hurry?

STORYTELLER. (*ignoring him, he keeps mumbling*) Hurry me home . . . hurry . . .

MARTIN. Don't you want to see what I have . . . my monster making stuff?

STORYTELLER. (*stops at once and turns toward* MARTIN) Your what?

MARTIN. You know. One of those kits with plastic molds and a rubbery goop that hardens.

STORYTELLER. (*worried*) You haven't made any monsters yet? Have you?

MARTIN. Just Torko here. (*He holds up the figure which is about eight inches tall.*) I call him Torko the Terrible, but his neck didn't come out too good. It's kind of weak, and his head keeps flopping over. See. (*He demonstrates the figure's loose head.*)

STORYTELLER. Oh my boots and bootles. I knew it. I knew it. I've got to get home if there's time. (*Exits right.*)

MARTIN. (*calling after him*) You too? I'm supposed to go to the dentist, and I'd like to make another monster first. I guess I better hurry. (*He turns and exits left as he came.*)

(*The curtain opens. There is a table and chair in the middle of the stage. The table is covered with a large cloth which hangs down on all sides to the floor.* MARTIN *enters left and puts his equipment on the table, propping* TORKO *up in full view. Even as he is doing all this his* MOTHER *calls from off-stage.*)

MOTHER. Martin. Martin. It's time to go. Clear away your things.

MARTIN. (*disappointed*) And I didn't even get started. (*calls to her*) Just a minute. (*He gathers up his materials and accidentally knocks* TORKO *off the table. He misses him and looks around on the table for him.*) Now where's that Torko?

MOTHER. Hurry, Martin.

MARTIN. (*grumbling to himself*) O.K. I'm coming. (*He looks around once again even on the floor.*) Gee, he was here a minute ago.

(MARTIN *exits left. The stage is dimmed and a bright ray of white light beams down on the table, and* TORKO, *now life-sized, crawls out from under it. At first he is stiff and it is difficult for him to get to his feet. During this action the* STORYTELLER, *still clutching his ledger, enters from the right and stands there watching. He holds one hand to his forehead in a gesture of despair. At the moment he is too frightened to speak.*)

TORKO. (*to the audience*) Well, this is better. I am big. I can talk. I can move my arms. (*he does so*) I can lift my legs. (*he does so*) And I can turn my head. (*As he does this his head flops backwards. He reaches up to straighten it.*) Oops! That might be a problem. Anyhow, I am real. I can go out into the world and make friends. (TORKO *exits right without noticing the* STORYTELLER.)

STORYTELLER. (*to the audience*) I told you . . . I told you something would happen. And I didn't get home in time. Now the only thing I can do is to follow that Torko and keep an eye on him. (*He exits mumbling.*) Oh my warts and wartles . . . trouble . . . trouble . . .

(*The curtain closes and remains closed as* TORKO *enters from the right. He goes down into the audience. The players who have been planted there scream and get up and run away.* TORKO *circles around and comes back onto the stage at the left as the curtain opens. The scene is in the park. There is a bench at the center of the stage where* LISA *sits with a couple of the girls.* OTHER CHILDREN *play with beach balls, hula hoops, or whatever else is appropriate. When* TORKO *enters there is screaming again.*)

LISA. (*who is only startled by the confusion*) What is it?

(*The* CHILDREN *run off except for* ROSIE *who lingers near the right exit.*)

LISA. Who frightened everybody away?

TORKO. (*sadly*) I did.

LISA. Why did they run when you came?

TORKO. I was going to ask you the same question.

LISA. Did you chase them?

TORKO. Oh no! I want to make friends. I'm called Torko the Terrible, but I'm really very well-mannered.

LISA. If you didn't chase them, you must have scared them by the way you look.

TORKO. Then why didn't you run?

LISA. (*laughs*) I'm never afraid of the looks of things, Torko. I can't see.

TORKO. Oh, I'm sorry. At least I suppose I should be sorry, but if you could see me, you probably would run too, and then I'd have no one to talk to.

LISA. I guess that's right. Do you look terrible?

TORKO. I don't know. I've never seen myself.

ROSIE. (*who has listened to the conversation and now moves over to* TORKO *and* LISA; *she speaks with a very superior air*) Well, I've seen you.

LISA. Oh, Rosie. There Torko, Rosie can see you and she didn't run.

ROSIE. Of course not. And I can certainly tell him what he looks like. He looks like a monster.

TORKO. I know I'm a monster, but what does a monster look like?

ROSIE. I should think you'd know, but since you don't there's a pond over there. (*She indicates a spot at the back of the stage on the right.*) You can see your reflection in the water.

(TORKO *crosses over to the pond and* ROSIE *turns to* LISA.)

LISA. He wants to make friends.

ROSIE. His appearance is definitely against it, but I read some place that all there is to making friends is to observe three rules. Be considerate. Be helpful. Be forgiving. I should think though that he'd want friends of his own kind. Monster friends.

TORKO. (*who has bent over the pond and caught his head in his hands as it flops forward now comes back to* LISA *and* ROSIE) I am different all right. But I don't mind being different as long as I'm real. I might as well tell you though, my head isn't on very good. Maybe I do look terrible when it flops around the way it does. Maybe I'll never have any friends.

LISA. I'll be your friend, Torko. How about you, Rosie?

ROSIE. I read some place that friends made in haste are a waste. But I'll take it under advisement.

LISA. I have to go now. My mother is waiting for me over by the big oak. I'll be back later.

TORKO. Do you need help?

ROSIE. (*laughs*) Lisa knows her way around the park better than I do.

LISA. Thanks just the same, Torko. Rosie, maybe you can help him find the others again. They won't run if they see you with him.

ROSIE. Oh, they'll come back. I read some place that people are always more curious than they are afraid.

TORKO. (*to* LISA) Will I see you again?

LISA. Of course. I come to this spot all the time. If you don't find me, just ask for Lisa.

(*As* LISA *exits left the* CHILDREN *begin to drift back.* STUMPY *throws a stone or two at* TORKO, *and* JOE *circles around and around making faces. The rest stay at a safe distance.*)

ROSIE. See. What did I tell you?

TORKO. (*to the children*) Don't run again. You don't have to look at me at first if you don't want to. (*He covers his face with his hands.*)

ROSIE. How about that? Rule number one . . . be considerate. You must have read the same book I did.

TORKO. You'll see how friendly I am. I know I look different . . . not like you, but I'm real. See how I can walk and turn my head.

(*As he does this his head flops backwards, and he has to take his hands from his face to hold it.*)

JOE. (*who has become bolder*) Your head is loose. What kind of a monster is that?

STUMPY. Yah. Yah. His head is loose. His head is loose.

TORKO. (*confused*) I think my neck's just too thin to hold it up. Maybe you can help me fix it. (*He walks toward* JOE *who now backs away. He trips and falls down.* TORKO *goes to him to help him up.*)

STUMPY. Look out, Joe. Don't let him grab you.

TORKO. I won't hurt you. (*He continues to help him.*)

ROSIE. There's the second rule all right. Be helpful. Maybe you don't need me at all.

JOE. (*looks at* TORKO *closely*) You're not as terrible as I thought you were. Stumpy, you keep those rocks to yourself. The monster's O.K.

(*The other* CHILDREN *come in closer now.*)

FLORA. He didn't chase us.

LUCY. He doesn't shake the ground when he walks.

SUSIE. He has a nice soft voice.

ROSIE. I read some place that a monster with a soft voice is a good monster.

STUMPY. (*coming up from the back where he had been throwing stones*) I'm sorry I threw stones.

TORKO. That's all right. I understand. (*He extends his hand.*) I'm Torko.

ROSIE. That does it. Rule number three. Be forgiving.

ALL. We're sorry we ran away from you.

TORKO. Then you'll be my friends. I don't have any friends . . . except Lisa.

ROSIE. We don't have any choice. You've passed the test. But didn't you have any friends where you came from

. . . monster friends? I read some place that one's first friends are chosen from one's own group.

TORKO. (*quickly*) But there wasn't anybody there like me. You see I'm *real.*

SUSIE. You keep saying that.

TORKO. Well, it's important.

LUCY. You really ought to have monster friends, but I don't know where to find any.

ROSIE. (*as usual with her superior air*) Well, I read some place that witches and ghosts and devils *and* monsters are all organized and they meet regularly.

LUCY. Maybe we can find them. Where do they meet?

ROSIE. (*for once a little embarrassed*) That's just it. I can't remember reading that.

JOE. Rosie, you read too much. Forget about the monsters. I know someone who'd like to know Torko. Martin!

TORKO. (*a little wary at the mention of the name*) Martin?

LUCY. Of course. Martin. He loves monsters. Let's find Martin.

(They start off left pulling TORKO *along with them. His head flops all around in his excitement, and when he frees his hands to hold it he lets the* CHILDREN *go on without him.)*

FLORA. *(as she exits left)* Hurry up, Torko.

SUSIE. *(following* FLORA*)* Hold on to your head, Torko, and run.

ROSIE. *(who has taken a very large book from her knapsack and has been thumbing through the pages, now moves toward the exit also)* You might as well, Torko. You've got nothing to lose, and maybe I can remember where I read about that monster meeting on the way. Come on . . . *(She exits motioning* TORKO *to follow.)*

(The CHILDREN *all exit leaving* TORKO *alone on the stage.)*

TORKO. *(to the audience)* Martin? Could it be my Martin? If it is, everything is ruined. He'll take me back. Maybe I could find where the monsters are meeting by myself. But I'd better hurry. *(*TORKO *exits right as the curtain closes.)*

(The STORYTELLER *enters from the wings at the left. He is out of breath and panting, but he still carries his ledger.)*

STORYTELLER. Oh my tears and toenails. That fellow is sure hard to keep up with. And did I hear him say he's going to find the monsters? You can see there's trouble ahead. That Torko doesn't even know what he is . . . not really. Torko the Terrible is going to have a terrible time. (*He exits mumbling.*) Terrible time . . .

(TORKO *comes out into the auditorium and runs back and forth and in circles and finally winds up on the stage at the left in front of the closed curtain. He is exhausted and his head is flopping uncontrollably. At last he collapses where he is standing as the curtain opens. There are signs posted near the various exits.* ←GOBLINS WITCHES→ GHOSTS↑ DEVILS↓ *On the back wall is a large banner:* MONSTER MEETING THE SIXTH TUESDAY OF EVERY MONTH. *The* MONSTERS *are standing in a semicircle and there is a babble of voices.* BIGWART, *the leader, wielding a large gavel, pounds the small table in front of him.*)

BIGWART. Order! Order! We'll never get anywhere this way. Order! (*When the group is quiet he continues.*) That's better. Now let's have the report on our popularity rating. Hagwart, where do we stand?

HAGWART. I don't think we're standing at all, sir. The ghosts are way up in the front with the witches and goblins close behind. We are definitely in the minority. Even the devils outnumber us this year. They've had a lot of free publicity lately.

BIGWART. I've heard about that. I understand they're not all red suits and horns and forked tails anymore. They're using disguises and that's sneaky. Ragwart, what are your plans for recruiting new members?

RAGWART. I have posted a bulletin, sir, asking for applicants, but we have to be so careful. There are a lot of pretenders around.

BIGWART. Maybe we should concentrate on quality then. It has come to my attention that a number of our number just aren't scary enough. Sagwart, that's your department.

SAGWART. The shape-up crew is adding fangs and bloody scars to all those who fail the terror test.

RAGWART. Some of the pretenders with their masks look better—I mean worse—than we do. How about extra eyes and webbed feet?

SAGWART. I'll make a note of it, but we are working forty-eight hours a day. You can't expect more than that.

BIGWART. Sagwart, there are only thirty-six hours in a day.

SAGWART. No wonder we're worn out.

(TORKO *sits up and begins to pound on the floor for attention.*)

BIGWART. (*to* RAGWART) Go check on that noise. (RAGWART *goes to* TORKO *as* BIGWART *continues.*) Zong, how about your committee on rules?

ZONG. We've drawn up a new set of standards for monster behavior. Practice sessions are held regularly in stomping and bellowing. We're pretty good in that department. (*He demonstrates by stomping in place and letting out wild howls.*)

(*During this speech* RAGWART *talks in inaudible tones to* TORKO *and gives him a scroll which unrolls to a great length.*)

BIGWART. (*to* ZONG) No need to show off, Zong. (*He then turns to* RAGWART *who has rejoined the group.*) Yes, Ragwart?

RAGWART. It could be a recruit, sir. Shall I bring him in?

BIGWART. Has he filled out an application?

RAGWART. He's doing it now, sir. He looks a little bit like you.

BIGWART. Then bring him in by all means. (RAGWART *exits.*) And while we're waiting let's get back to you, Zong. What else are you doing?

ZONG. I myself am teaching daily classes in chasing and grabbing, sir . . . very popular.

(RAGWART *enters with* TORKO *and hands* BIGWART *the application.* TORKO *stands holding his head.*)

BIGWART. (*to* TORKO) You are applying for membership in the Great League of Galactic Monsters?

TORKO. (*very meekly*) If that means you'd be my friends, then I am.

BIGWART. Hmmm. Not much in the way of a voice, but we could work on that. (*He unrolls the scroll and looks at the application.*) Torko the Terrible. It says here you frightened children in the park but later made friends with them. That's a little irregular.

HAGWART. Questionable, I'd say.

ZONG. Ask him about chasing and grabbing.

TORKO. Is that necessary?

SAGWART. He sounds definitely substandard.

RAGWART. Maybe even a pretender.

TORKO. A pretender? You mean . . .

BIGWART. That's right . . . pretending to be a monster.

TORKO. Don't say that. That's the one thing that's important. I'm real. I've got to be real. (*In his excitement he takes his hands from his head and it flops around wildly.*)

BIGWART. What in the world is the matter with your head?

TORKO. I'm afraid it's loose, sir.

ALL. Loose! ! !

BIGWART. That's bad.

HAGWART. Inspection! I call for inspection.

ALL. Second the motion.

(*They all converge on* TORKO *to inspect him. One drops to the floor to look at his feet. Another moves his head back and forth. Another pokes at his arms and legs.*)

TORKO. (*frightened*) Don't hurt me, please.

BIGWART. Nobody's hurting you. There's always inspection before a vote.

RAGWART. Vote! Vote! I call for the vote.

MONSTERS. (*The* MONSTERS *step back into place, and one by one they shout out their vote.*) Reject! Reject! Reject!

ALL. Unanimous reject.

TORKO. Does that mean we can't be friends after all?

BIGWART. You must understand. We don't mean to be unfriendly, but there is so much fraud in the world today.

RAGWART. So much dishonesty.

SAGWART. So much pretense.

HAGWART. All front . . .

ZONG. And no substance.

BIGWART. We have to be very careful who we let into the organization. There are certain requirements.

TORKO. (*sighs*) I guess I understand.

BIGWART. Hagwart, show him out.

(HAGWART *and several others grab* TORKO *and carry him off left.*)

BIGWART. (*calling after them*) If we ever change the rules, we'll get in touch with you, Torko. (*to the audience*) Too bad. He did look a little like me. (*Quick curtain.*)

(*The* CHILDREN *come out from the left in front of the closed curtain. There is a babble of voices.*)

STUMPY. Where's Torko?

SUSIE. I thought he was right behind us.

LUCY. I wonder where we'll find Martin?

FLORA. Probably back at the park.

(*They exit right as* ROSIE *enters left. She holds a big book and is searching for something in it.*)

ROSIE. I still think we should have tried to find the monsters. (ROSIE *exits right as* TORKO *enters from the left.*)

TORKO. (*to the audience*) Now I don't know where to go. They've probably found Martin, and it's all over. Maybe if I can get back to Lisa she'll help me.

(*The curtain opens on the park scene with* LISA *back on the bench.* TORKO *moves into the scene.*)

TORKO. Lisa. I'm sure glad you're here.

LISA. Torko? What's the matter? Didn't you make friends?

TORKO. I made friends all right but now I'm afraid I'm going to lose them. I found some other monsters too, but to tell you the truth they frightened me.

LISA. (*laughs*) Frightened you, Torko? That's funny.

(*There is noise offstage right and the* CHILDREN *enter.*)

JOE. There he is with Lisa.

FLORA. Where did you go, Torko? We lost you.

STUMPY. Well, we've found him again, and look . . . (*points off left*) Here comes Martin. Rosie must have found him.

(ROSIE *enters with* MARTIN *and* TORKO *puts both hands over his face.*)

MARTIN. What's all the excitement?

JOE. We've got someone we want you to meet. (*He pulls* TORKO*'s hands from his face.*) You don't have to hide from Martin. He makes monsters. (*laughs*) Not big ones like you though.

MARTIN. (*crosses to* TORKO) Say, let me look at you. It can't be . . . but it is. You're Torko.

TORKO. No I'm not. No I'm not. (*He is frightened.*)

LISA. But there's no need for Torko to be afraid of Martin.

MARTIN. Well, there's no need for anybody to be afraid of Torko. He's only a toy.

TORKO. (*starts to cry*) That's not true. (*his head flops around*)

MARTIN. You know it's true, Torko. I don't know what happened to you to make you grow, but see, your head's loose. You're my Torko all right.

TORKO. (*crying harder*) You've spoiled everything. Go away. Go away, all of you.

ALL (*except* ROSIE *and* LISA *and* MARTIN). A toy! He's only a toy! (*They shrink away from him and exit.*)

MARTIN. (*bewildered*) I don't understand any of this. (*to* TORKO) I wish I could help, but I couldn't even get your head on right.

TORKO. (*still crying*) Never mind. Just go away.

(MARTIN *exits in a kind of daze.*)

LISA. Don't cry, Torko.

TORKO. The monsters wouldn't have me either. I've lost all my friends.

LISA. Not all of them, Torko. I'm still your friend.

TORKO. And I wasn't ever real at all.

LISA. You'll always be real to me. Remember I see things other people can't.

ROSIE. I read some place that everyone has to be exactly what he is, and that's a fact.

TORKO. I suppose that means I have to go back.

LISA. I suppose. Come on, I'll walk a way with you. (LISA *and* TORKO *exit leaving* ROSIE *alone on the stage with her books.*)

ROSIE. (*thumbing through the pages of a big book, she mumbles*) Monsters . . . no . . . toy monsters . . . toys . . . real . . . There's got to be something to cover this. If I could only find it. (*Keeps on mumbling and turning the pages as the curtain falls.*)

(TORKO *enters left in front of the closed curtain and* LISA'*s voice is heard from offstage.*)

LISA. Good-by, Torko. And don't worry.

(TORKO *walks very slowly toward the right exit when suddenly* ROSIE *calls from offstage left.*)

ROSIE. Wait . . . (*She enters carrying a large dictionary. She runs across to* TORKO.) Wait, Torko! Wait. (*She opens the book to the place she has marked.*) I found it. It was right here in the dictionary all the time. (*she reads*) Real. It means genuine, authentic. Torko, you are a genuine, authentic, toy, and there's nothing wrong with that. . . . You are real after all. Come on now.

(*She pulls* TORKO, *who has brightened up a little, off right.*) And remember, toys are very important. (*They exit.*)

(*The curtain rises on the room of the first scene. There is the same dimmed light.* ROSIE *and* TORKO *enter right.*)

ROSIE. Your worries are all over, Torko. Just be what you are.

TORKO. I will, Rosie, and thank you.

(ROSIE *exits and* TORKO *stands for a minute very tall and straight and without holding onto his head.*)

TORKO. Real. Genuine. Authentic. And it's a lot easier this way.

(*He crawls back under the table as the* STORYTELLER *enters left. He is bedraggled . . . his cap is down over one eye, he has lost one of his boots and the ledger, which he still has with him, is held carelessly by one cover.*)

STORYTELLER. Oh my tears and toenails. I didn't think I'd ever catch up with him this time. I can tell you this is one day I'm glad to be finished with. Still, Torko's story did turn out better than I thought it would. Anything could have happened, you know. Just don't expect me to be around next year. The agency's going to have to get themselves another boy. Oh my warts and wartles . . . what a day. (*He exits left as the curtain closes.*)

SUGGESTIONS

Everything is pretty well spelled out for you here. The storyteller, as the script indicates, should be a gnomelike character, a creature of a fairytale world. He has the floppy peaked cap, of course, and tiny spectacles, plus boots, because in the end he has lost one of them. Maybe he could have bright striped stockings, one of which we see in the final scene. The stool could be a small stepladder, and the ledger should be a big one.

Torko, the toy figure, must be a replica of Torko full-sized. You won't have any trouble finding an old doll with a movable head that Martin can twist to show that it is loose. If you used a large ice cream carton or any other cylindrical container for the head of the full-sized Torko, you could fasten it securely around the player's neck and then cut out a round section for his face. You might weight the top of the carton so that it gets off balance easily.

Give Rosie great saucer-like glasses and a knapsack, school bag, or something of the sort in which to carry her books. It will be better if she can hang it over her shoulder or back to leave her arms free.

The other children, including Lisa and Martin, are just children. They might even use their own names if they wish, but each person should have a particular characteristic. The cast will have ideas about that.

The monsters can be whatever you make of them—wild. Bigwart, remember, looks a little like Torko. Why not give him a carton head too, except that he is able to hold his head in place. Each monster should also have a distinct personality. Bigwart, the leader, is authoritative. Hagwart is apologetic. Ragwart is bossy. Sagwart is a little slow in mind and movement. Zong is definitely a showoff. And don't forget the signs.

The sets for the play can be more elaborate than indicated. It would be great if Torko could climb *out* and *in* a window, but no matter. The ray of light could be provided by a flashlight if no spotlight is available. And one last thing . . . be sure no one walks where the pond is in the park scene. It might be wise to mark it off. On the other hand maybe it would be funny if someone falls in. You can then add a line about being a dummy not to see the water. Have fun with it.

PART VII

IMPROVISATION

IMPROVISATION

. . . no planning ahead . . .

To improvise means to invent, compose, or recite without preparation, and it is very popular these days. It is often used in school to work out social problems. It is used on playgrounds and in recreational activities. Even television actors have tried it out on nation-wide networks. It is also used in games. Do you remember charades? Or how about "Lemonade—What's your trade?—Show us some, if you're not afraid." That was pantomime, of course, but improvisation nonetheless; performances made up on the spot. It was great fun because you were part of the action.

Improvisation should definitely be a part of any book on dramatic art. What a wonderful ice-breaker at rehearsal time or at the early sessions of acting classes or workshops. Toss out a subject or situation or a point of disagreement to a number of players and see what develops. Use pantomime or dialogue or both. Try to resolve the issue in some manner or at least come to an acceptable finish.

How about a person, already late for an appointment, caught in stand-still traffic. What does he do? Or two hikers who cannot agree on which path to take down the mountain. What could happen? You must know dozens of problems you could suggest at the drop of a hat. That kind of acting exercise would certainly be worthwhile.

To improvise before an invited audience, however, is another matter. It isn't easy to come up with action and dialogue extemporaneously, especially if you are trying to provide entertainment for parents and friends. Be sure your group can do it. Of course, if your audience knows what kind of performance is to be given and is even willing to be drawn into it, to participate, you could involve them in some way in order to hold their interest. Let them guess what you are doing if it's pantomime. Or encourage volunteers from the crowd to join you.

Do remember, though, that most people who are invited to a show expect, and have a right to expect, entertainment that has been prepared for them, entertainment that has been planned and organized and rehearsed.

And that's what this book is all about.

VIRGINIA BRADLEY

Childhood enthusiasm for backyard play production and an equal fondness for putting words together led VIRGINIA BRADLEY to the theater arts and English departments of the University of Nebraska. After a period of teaching and an acting stint with a touring repertory company, she abandoned career for marriage and a family.

The urge to write, however, persisted and Virginia Bradley has produced adult short stories, humor, articles, and light verse along with plays for Cub Scouts, Brownies, and the schoolroom. For a number of years, she has directed writing workshops for the adult division of the Los Angeles schools. Her books include *Holidays on Stage: A Festival of Special Occasion Plays* and *Stage Eight*, a collection of original one-act plays, as well as young adult novels.

Mrs. Bradley lives with her family in Santa Monica, California.